Southern Fried White Trash
by Carole Townsend

Printed in the United States of America

Crabgrass Publishing, LLC

ISBN 978-0-615-53367-4

Southern-Fried White Trash

Carole Townsend

Crabgrass Publishing, LLC

Publishing

www.crabgrasspublishing.com

Dedication

This book is dedicated to Southerners, to our roots, our families and our homes. It is dedicated to the way we were raised and to those who raised us. It is written with the utmost love and respect for everything held dear by these quirky and charming people.

It is also dedicated to my husband Marc, who encouraged me to live my dream, and to my children, who inspire me to create.

Any resemblance in these accounts, real or implied, to either guilty or innocent parties, is probably right on the money and completely intentional. How else can we sort all this out and still share a private laugh?

--Carole

Credits

Thanks to Dana K. Walters for sharing her very pregnant belly with us for the cover. What a great sport!

Thanks to James Dempsey for his photographic genius.

Preface

I've thought about this a lot, how to begin this book that's been inside my head for nearly fifty years. It only makes sense to begin where I began, growing up in the South. My childhood home was in Doraville, Georgia, a sleepy suburb of Atlanta.

I was one of four children. Three of us lived at home with our parents; my oldest sister had already married and moved to San Diego with her husband. My parents were probably the most mismatched couple on earth; Mom was a tough and dare I say, unhappy woman. She loved her children but only knew to raise us by rules, not by heart. My dad knew even less about raising children, traveling for months at a time and playing the laid-back Yang to Mom's Yin when he was at home, oil to her water. In truth he was her fifth child, and he frustrated her greatly.

They were parents before "parent" became a verb. They were both true Southerners, though. Mom grew up in southern Virginia, and Dad hailed from Tennessee. In spite of the sometimes chaos and constant dysfunction of our home, one of the things that stands out most in my memory is my mother's sense of propriety, her sense of what ought to be done in any given situation. Not a woman to whom mothering and nurturing came easily, she often leaned on "manners maven" Emily Post for direction. She owned several volumes penned by Ms. Post, and I believe she could quote chapter and verse if push came to shove (as it often did). Her world revolved around her perception of etiquette and propriety, two concepts that are rasping their last dying breaths in our generation, I'm afraid.

For example, my mother was positively obsessed with the proper placement of utensils on a dining table. "Salad fork, dinner fork, plate, knife, spoon," she would recite, and all had to be placed exactly one inch in from the edge of the table. I was always puzzled by her fascination with the arrangement of flatware. Dinner time at our house was, on a good day, ordinary. Often, it was punctuated by sibling silliness, parental sparring, last-minute guests, things like that.

When we did go out to eat dinner as a family, we usually went to Bonanza, my parents' favorite family dining haunt. Bonanza was a roll-your-sleeves-up, all-you-can-eat, steak and burger place not far from our house. Their flatware came rolled up in a paper napkin and sealed with a glued-together paper napkin ring. I used to wonder what my mom, channeling Ms. Post, thought about that.

I wisely never asked the question.

Looking back, I often try to see how my life has prepared me for my life. In a way, I suppose it has. I think (no, I know) that my sense of humor sprouted like a defiant little seedling during my elementary school years and grew taller and stronger during high school strictly out of necessity. A fat girl catches the brunt of every small-minded joke that small-minded people can muster.

I sometimes wonder what it would be like to catch up to some of those people from my early years, to see where their lives have taken them--prison maybe, or a single-wide in an unkempt trailer park. What's that saying about "he who laughs last?" Anyway, I suppose my childhood wasn't unlike thousands of others. And I am grateful for that sense of humor.

I grew up to be a mom, a happily married wife, and a writer. I took a detour getting here via a successful marketing career and several other distractions--principally two previous husbands--but where I am now is what matters.

I love words. I love how they look on paper and how they sound in people's heads. I love how they mean one thing to me and quite another to you.

I have come to learn that "different" isn't necessarily "bad." My siblings and I are different because of our genetic makeup, just as we are similar because of our shared wiring. It's one of the fascinating things I have learned in this desperate fifty-year marathon. Different is not only good; it is the background on which we lay our own experiences. It's what gives us a point of reference.

Now add "Southern" to the mix. I love everything about the South. I love the mild winters and the smotheringly hot summers. I love dogwoods and magnolias and azaleas. I love a southern drawl--a genuine one, that is. Please don't try to imitate it; I've never heard anyone pull it off without sounding like they're eating oatmeal while recovering from extensive oral surgery. A true Southern accent is measured, warm, and wise. Many mistake it for mental sluggishness or just downright ignorance, but I'm willing to bet those same people have had their pockets picked clean by someone with a Southern accent: never knew what hit them. Don't mistake a southern drawl for anything other than what it is--pure buttery charm.

I am particularly fond of Southern mannerisms and colloquialisms. I love the rules of propriety and etiquette, passed on for generations and practiced by true Southern folks. Knowing these rules is akin to belonging to a secret club. Outsiders neither practice nor understand nor even appreciate them, but we Southerners hold them dear.

I love the word "ma'am." It has so many meanings depending on its use, but they all boil down to the same thing: "I see that you're a woman, and as such you deserve a nod in your direction, Ma'am." In my mind, it has nothing to do with age or hierarchy. It has to do with tradition and civility, and I love it.

I love how little children in the South refer respectfully to an elderly woman as "Miss so-and-so."

I love the gracious way of life here in the South. It's not a slow pace here anymore; even so, one can still sense a gracefulness and quiet pride in the living. Atlanta has spread her skirts to include literally hundreds of cultures, a multiplicity of races, uncountable religions, even a variety of sexual preferences, but she is still the capital of the South and queen of all that comes with that distinction.

A case in point: Who else but a Southerner could splash branch water into three fingers of bourbon, stir in some sugar, throw in a leaf, and call the concoction something as lyrical as a mint julep? It's carbed-up liquor, but "mint julep" sounds so cooling and musical. So

Southern. Yes, I'm fixin' to raise a mint julep in honor of all things Southern.

Growing up Southern in a generation that saw the divorce rate double, witnessed the onset of drive-thru funerals, and gave glittery new meaning to the word "grill" made my own upbringing a stark contrast to much of the rest of the world. And therein lies the premise of this book.

True Southerners have a unique and quirky way of approaching pretty much everything in life, thus giving everything in life a little more color. The South has given rise to some delightfully colorful characters (Paula Deen and Jeff Foxworthy, to name a couple). It was home to Rosa Parks and Dr. Martin Luther King, and it was also home to segregationist Georgia governors Lester Maddox and George Wallace. The South is a multi-fragranced, discordantly melodious paradox that has birthed both greatness and shame, beauty and tragedy.

Only here have so much tradition, progress, history, angst, and hope clashed, ricocheted, and tumbled together to create the smooth, beautiful rock we Southerners call home. From all those contrasts, a long legacy of rules and imperatives have evolved. Suffice it to say that if you were born here, you get it. If you weren't, you don't.

Table of Contents

Southerners, White Trash, Rednecks, and Other Folks

Let's begin with the basics:

Southerner: "a native or inhabitant of the South; especially a native or resident of the southern part of the United States" (as defined by the *Merriam-Webster Dictionary*). Contrary to widespread opinion, Southerners are for the most part bright, well-educated, and free-thinking people.

white trash: "used as a disparaging term for a white person or white people perceived as being lazy and ignorant" (as defined by *The Free Dictionary* by Farlex). Typically, these people also have atrocious taste, are quite often poor, and have no earthly idea of propriety, etiquette, or marginally acceptable manners.

redneck: "sometimes disparaging: a white member of the Southern rural laboring class" (as defined by the *Merriam-Webster Dictionary*). Case studies have, however, documented instances of rednecks living in New York, Washington State, and even California. Being a redneck is as much a state of mind as it is about a geographic area, apparently. **other folks**: everybody else.

For the purposes of this book, I plan to focus mainly on several white-trash case studies from the point of view of a proper Southerner.

The last thing I want to do in this book is to ridicule or denigrate any group or socio-economic class that makes up part of the population of this wonderful country we all call home. Variety, differences, colorful people, and perspectives from all angles make up a fascinating world, and I enjoy that world very much.

Many Americans of notoriety descended from what's known as "poor white trash," including Abraham Lincoln and Britney Spears (by some accounts). I have no personal knowledge of either person's lineage or upbringing, and I'm not sure I ever read where Mr. Lincoln shaved his head, then shoved an umbrella through a car window to the delight of the paparazzi, all while chewing a giant wad of Bubble Yum, but again I am no expert. Suffice it to say that if it's good enough for Abe, it ought to be good enough for me.

My problem is that I get hung up on the perception, on the rules of Southern etiquette, that were drilled into my head as a kid. That perception, laid against the background that is the reality of the world in which we live, always makes me laugh. In truth, I suppose I am laughing at myself more than at anyone else. Did I really think, as I grew up, that people would follow any prescribed set of rules, would, least of all, play by the rules I thought appropriate? Yes, I suppose I did. I wrote this book as much to poke fun at myself as at anyone or any group of people. The truth of the matter is that we all have a little bit of white trash in us. If one is squeezed hard enough it'll come out, trust me.

I also have to find humor in the fact that, even today, I often measure my life experiences by that antiquated Southern yardstick marked by manners, civilities, and protocol. Does it even apply anymore? In general I'd have to say that, sadly, no, it doesn't. But that doesn't stop me from clutching it tightly just the same. The contrast between the expectations of a true Southern woman and the stark reality of the world outside that sheltered circle (in which most of us now live) makes for some pretty funny situations.

The South is famous for its subcultures. Some of these groups blur boundaries and run into the north, midwest, or west, but one in particular--rednecks--is indigenous to the South. The term *redneck,* by definition, refers to a member of the rural laboring class, more often in the South. Now to be sure, every state in the union is home to a similar faction. In some states they're called "hillbillies," in others "hicks" or "crackers." The list goes on and on, but you get the idea.

In reality, being called a redneck is not necessarily a bad thing, unless of course you are not one. In fact, it's considered a compliment in some circles, like being called a "good ol' boy." Most politicians in the South fall under the "good ol' boy" category, and some fall into both the "redneck" and "good ol' boy" categories. Unless rednecks move out of the South as the result of a job transfer or an attempt to evade an ex-spouse and the ensuing monthly payments, they are almost always found living right here below the Mason-Dixon line.

White trash is another subculture, and this group is by no means found only in the South. You know the type: those people who bring air horns and cow bells to graduations. Those people who can't marry the daddy of their current baby because they're still common-law married to the daddy of the last one, and he's still in prison. The ones who make a point of discussing, in graphic detail, at least one bodily function at every meal or gathering. Yes, you know the type.

A hardy bunch, white-trash people can survive and even thrive pretty much anywhere on the planet. It's been said that a nuclear war will obliterate everything on earth except cockroaches and white trash. Some say the two are interchangeable. To be clear, calling someone "white trash" implies that they are a member of an inferior or underprivileged white social group. While white trash folks are not found only in the South, I will say that our strain of the breed puts an interesting spin on this subculture. Don't be offended by the term *white trash*; true white trash is proud to be just that.

An offshoot of the white-trash subculture is the newer group referred to as "trailer trash." I believe trailer trash can be found in as many locations as can white trash, but I'd have to check my facts on that. Being called trailer trash is much worse than being called white trash in my mind, although I'm not sure why--probably because I'm claustrophobic, although I don't think the term refers solely to a type of dwelling. Neither name is delivered as a compliment, but again, when the shoe fits, it's worn proudly.

Those of us raised to be "proper" Southerners are never quite sure of how to deal with rednecks, white trash, et al. We're a dying breed, we Southerners. That may be for the best, I don't know, but we are. Back in the days of my great-grandparents, the South was just emerging from a dark and desolate era. Life was often hard, both socially and economically. There was discord, shame, and bruised pride. But there were also beautiful treasures here, the underpinnings of a gracious and orderly life that many couldn't bear to extinguish. So our forefathers (and mothers) preserved and treasured behaviors that bespoke a gentler, more civilized time. Then they passed them down to their children, and so on, and so on.

I'm talking about the unwritten rules of propriety, of the way things just were. I'm talking about gentility and manners and practices that lived only here in the South. I'm talking about opening doors for women. I'm talking about sending thank-you notes for kindnesses both big and small. I'm talking about "please" and "thank you," "Ma'am" and "Sir." I'm talking about not wearing white before the Kentucky Derby or after Labor Day. Ever.

These customs have attenuated, evolved, somewhat dissolved, yes. But they still live here. You have to look for them, listen for them. Transplants have diluted our Southern way of life (though it's true: we still welcome pretty much everyone). The breakneck pace we all must keep just to keep our heads above water is the real enemy. It's hard to be truly courteous when you're late, with everything, all the time.

What amuses me is how we Southerners deal with this contrast, proof that a sense of humor is the first thing you should pack in your Southerner's Survival Kit should you ever come visit.

Every event in life has a proper reaction, at least here in the South. (If you don't believe me, ask my mother.) If a friend or relative passes away, you bring a casserole or Bundt cake to a surviving family member's home. If you receive a wedding invitation, you RSVP, buy a thoughtful gift, and attend the ceremony. If someone has a baby, you follow the casserole/Bundt cake action plan. For some reason, a death and a birth both warrant casseroles and cakes. Weddings, on the other hand, do not. Go figure.

These rules and prescribed reactions may sound silly to outsiders, but to us they help make sense of life. They help us keep things orderly and in order. They also account for the fact that there are a lot of fat people hanging around maternity wards and funeral homes, but that's another matter entirely.

My skewed perception of life and how people ought to behave continued right through college. I attended a private university in Nashville, then a school that comes as close to Ivy League as you're going to get in the Deep

South. All the proprieties with which I grew up were alive and well among both populations. There was money, there was gentility, there was a bit of snobbishness, and there was shelter.

It wasn't until I reached my mid-twenties that I came face-to-face with two indisputable facts:

> 1. Life is divided into phases and marked by monumental events, such as weddings and deaths, and
> 2. People show their true colors during those very same events.

When plunged into one of these significant life events, every thread woven into a person's upbringing, everything they've been taught (and everything they haven't) surfaces. As I have come to learn, the result is revealing and not always flattering.

The accounts that follow are all actual experiences I've shared with acquaintances, friends, and family in my life. I have weighed the wisdom of whether to share these anecdotes, for fear of offending the involved parties. I have to say that if you find half the humor in them today that I found when they happened, the risk is well worth it. Those days on which we lose the ability to laugh at ourselves are always sad ones, indeed. So to all of you whose stories I am sharing, I thank you. You have truly enriched my life, whether you know it or not. To those of you who are reading these stories for the first time, I have a hunch that you'll relate to at least one of them, because no matter how crazy you sometimes think you are, there's always someone crazier within your line of sight. You'll likely figure that out at your next family function.

Weddings

I met the most charming couple recently, Lucinda and Burt, both of whom I'd guess are in their mid-sixties. She is about as Southern as a woman can get; she has the accent, the mannerisms, that quirky presence that both charms and puzzles many people. She has that talent that still amazes me, the ability to make you feel like you're her long-lost friend, even if you just met her. She is also an accomplished cook, well known in the Carolinas for her culinary talents. She and her husband, Burt, were preparing for their youngest daughter's wedding, which would be taking place in a mere two months.

Lucinda and I met at a book signing. We hit it off right away, and my husband clicked with Burt. The very day we met, she and I were talking about the grand details of what promised to be an impressive affair. The wedding was to be held at a famous winery and inn here in Georgia. Lucinda's taste and obvious love of tradition showed in even the smallest details. But then, from within the comfortable and gracious ambience of Lucinda's love of tradition and good taste, I found my mind wandering to a few of the more memorable weddings I've attended. Taste and a love of tradition are properly anticipated for some weddings, like that of Lucinda's daughter, but throw in a family feud, a gene pool that's dangerously shallow in places, at least one visit from the cops, and an unplanned pregnancy or two, and you've got yourself quite another version of a wedding--the white-trash version.

Weddings in any culture are important events fraught with meaning and emotion. They give us the hope and promise of true love. They blend all that we believe and hold dear into one beautiful ceremony--family, marriage, reverence for a God who ordains the union, and, of course, great food.

Throughout my childhood and well into young adulthood, I recall the weddings I attended as being lavish, extravagant affairs. I remember the rituals and traditions. I remember, once I was old enough to consider the possibility that I might one day marry, thumbing through bridal magazines and talking with my girlfriends about our own "someday" weddings. We'd conjure up images of magnificent gowns, huge, richly decorated churches, hundreds and hundreds of guests and of course the most handsome groom. We'd talk about the flowers, the sumptuous banquet and even the music.

And we just knew without a doubt, as surely as the sun rises in the east, that what we imagined would be the reality. Right?

Tiny

Before I embark on this first of these true-life accounts of several strange weddings I've attended, let me say right out of the gate that I have changed or outright omitted some names in the retelling. While I find humor and irony in these accounts, the actual participants might not. So, I've altered the names in the service of good stories, because a good story is a treasure and begs to be told, don't you think?

Not long after I graduated college, I was invited to attend the wedding of a close childhood friend. She moved to Columbia, Tennessee, when we were still teens, but we had stayed in touch over the years. My friend was marrying a young man from Ringgold, Georgia. They had only known each other for three short months, but they had met on a church singles trip to Biloxi, Mississippi. It had been love at first sight. The wedding was to take place in Columbia that very August.

Three friends made the trip to Tennessee with me late that hot, sticky summer. We were all so young, so full of romantic ideals, so convinced that the notions of "soulmates" and "love at first sight" were the real and naturally guiding forces of human destiny. Armed with those notions and our carefully marked back issues of *BRIDE* magazine, we checked into our hotel and settled in.

My girlfriends and I arrived at the church early the next morning to help with the final wedding preparations. In truth, we just wanted to be near our friend in case she needed us. This was such a big day for her, and we wanted to do whatever we could to make sure it was perfect, just as we had always dreamed.

The church was charming, a picture postcard. The sanctuary was buzzing with activity--florists, nervous assistants--and everything seemed to be coming together very nicely. Having seen that there were no disasters to fend off, no fires to be put out, the four of us began making our way to where the bride might be, or at least to where we might find her mother and sisters. Southern weddings, you understand, typically take place entirely in the same church building--everything from preparation to staging to the ceremony to the reception.

Now these old churches are often mazes, labyrinths, veritable catacombs of complexity, with steeples. Some are so old that they've been remodeled, refurbished, and expanded countless times over the years. It didn't take us long to get lost, and fifteen minutes into the adventure we found ourselves listening for signs of life just to find our way back to people.

As we wandered, we heard crying, far off at first but getting louder by the moment--a little distressing but at least a sound--and we followed it. As we got closer to the source of the sound, we realized that it was not crying that we heard but outright wailing, the sound of loss and heartbreak typically reserved for an untimely death or some other tragic loss.

Following twisting, narrow hallways for another minute or two, we came upon a large room obviously decorated for a wedding celebration. We surmised that we had found the reception hall and went in. Judging by the volume of the caterwauling, this room also happened to be the source of the distressing sound. Curious beyond the point of turning back, the four of us followed the agonized crying to a bench in the very back of the hall. On it sat the groom's father, the apparent wailer. Around him stood a few people, patting his arm and whispering what sounded like heartfelt condolences.

Perplexed, we discreetly asked bystanders what the matter was, why the man was crying. Everyone seemed too embroiled, too immediately invested in the proceedings to answer. Finally, a woman with a beehive hairdo piled frightfully high and shellacked into submission walked past our little huddled group. She was shaking her head and muttering to herself. Touching her arm, I pursued our question: "What on earth is the matter with that man? Isn't he the father of the groom? Why is he crying like that?"

In a whispered tone typically reserved for funeral parlors and bathroom stall confidences, this woman prepared to share with me the horrible events that had taken place just that morning. I quickly gathered my friends and we sat stone still, bracing ourselves for the worst possible news. Maybe the groom had been hit by a bus. Maybe the man's wife had passed away that morning. His angst was that deep. We held our breath.

"Tiny's dead," she whispered, raising one eyebrow as though she had just shared a long-buried family secret. "He ate some rat poison left out at the barn. They found him this morning, stiff as a board."

"Tiny?" I gasped. "His child? Grandchild? Oh, how terrible!" I exclaimed as we horrified friends all clasped hands and uttered a gasp in unison.

"No child, his dog. His hunting dog. His pride and joy. You know, Tiny!" she whispered again, wiggling her eyebrows up and down dramatically as if the revelation of the dog's identity might bring upon us a shared epiphany of recognition capable of ripping the heavens in half.

I digested this for a moment, then looked at my friends to be sure I had heard her right. They looked to be busily digesting too, checking my expression to verify that they had heard what she said.

I looked over at the groom's father. He was sobbing, his whole body shaking, and people who appeared to be family members and devastated friends surrounded him in comfort. I could only catch scraps of what was being said, but here goes:

"He was a good dawg, never was no trouble to nobody."

"Best huntin' dawg in the state...never be another one like him."

". . . proper burial...only right. . . ."

What? A proper burial? I looked around to be sure we were at the right church. Yes, there was a photo of the lovely couple right next to the green punch fountain and a mountain of pale pink *petit fours*. This had to be the place.

Confused and a little disoriented, we left the hall and headed in the general direction of the sanctuary, as best as we could make it out without a compass. I remembered things being more under control up there, more what I expected to see at a sweet Southern wedding. We walked in silence, each chewing on what we had just heard. That man, who looked to be as sane as anyone else, was absolutely devastated over the loss of a hunting dog? On his son's wedding day? Wasn't he over-reacting? Weren't there more important things going on all around him? I mean, I am a tried-and-true dog lover, but this was bizarre even to me.

This would be a good time to explore the relationship between "country" Southerners (sometimes referred to as rednecks) and their dogs. True country Southerners are very much like rednecks. They're from the south, but they differ from "city" southerners, who can also be rednecks. City southerners treat their dogs like little people. Their dogs go to salons, they stay in doggie bed-and-breakfasts, they dine from monogrammed pewter dishes, and they have their own wardrobe. Some even have therapists and play dates. They have the run of the homes in which they live. Country Southerners (aka rednecks) are appalled by all that. Their dogs have purposes. They have jobs. A dog could be a cattle dog, a guard dog or, as in Tiny's case, a hunting dog. They are rarely allowed indoors--considered unsanitary and dulling of the animal's primary instincts. Even so, true country folks revere their best dogs almost to the point of worshipping them. They are family (and in some cases I mean that literally, a point I could make with amazing examples, but those are not for the purposes of this story). In either instance, the city or the country setting, the death of a dog (not a pet mind you, but a furry, four-legged family member) is devastating. In this particular instance, with his son's nuptials and his beloved Tiny's demise, this poor man simply could not cope.

We stepped back into the bustling sanctuary, still chewing on what Beehive had shared, just in time to see a heavyset, no-nonsense-looking woman, apparently the weeping man's wife, carry a photo to the front of the church. She busied herself placing it just so among the candles and flower arrangements there, pausing every few seconds to dab at her eyes.

She stepped back to admire her handiwork, and I could see that she had lovingly placed an 8x10 glossy photograph of Tiny on the altar, front and center. Dabbing at her eyes and nose again with a hanky, the woman sat on the first pew and began to sob. All the busy workers in the sanctuary stopped and whispered in awe and reverence, an apparent verbal salute to Tiny. Sniffles and hugs followed and a couple of people scurried from the room, unable to contain their emotions.

I don't think the somber nature of the woman's gesture fully registered with me, because so help me God I started laughing. I'm not sure what came over me. It horrifies me to this day, but it happened just the same. As I recall, I laughed so hard that I couldn't catch my breath. I have since come to understand that I do that when I'm uncomfortable or nervous. My friends were trying in vain to stifle their giggles, but my hysterical laughter only made them follow suit. I could feel the others' eyes on me. I could feel their disbelief and horror at my complete lack of compassion and respect for Tiny the Amazing Hunting Dog. And still I laughed. A lot, and for quite a while. I felt like Alice in Wonderland at the bottom of the rabbit hole, only this hole looked like a little country church with a photo of a rock-star bloodhound on the altar.

Now, I have been to country-club weddings and exotic-destination weddings. I have witnessed weddings on yachts and weddings in hot-air balloons. I have been to simple little Baptist affairs with no alcohol, and I have been to weddings where the food and alcohol kept coming for days. But this was the first wedding I had ever attended during which funeral preparations for a dog were discussed over Lime Delight punch and dainty cucumber sandwiches.

Think I'm kidding? The ceremony was beautiful by the way, but somehow odd and a little offbeat. The groom was noticeably shaken by Tiny's untimely passing. Although no one had said so in my hearing, I'm pretty sure he had been drinking before the ceremony, strictly out of grief of course. He fell down in a heap on the altar twice before saying, "I do." The bride--our dear, disillusioned friend--was very noticeably upset over the groom's . . . grief. His entire family spoke in hushed tones about whether they'd be able to get the preacher to deliver Tiny's eulogy on such short notice. In fact, the wedding for them had become an afterthought, a bothersome task they had to endure before they could begin to grieve properly. They discussed the appropriateness of burying Tiny in the family plot (wait a minute, aren't there laws?).

And one young gentleman, who shall remain nameless but whose orange-striped tube socks peeked out from under the legs of his beige polyester suit when he crossed his legs, asked me to accompany him to the funeral as his date. I couldn't help staring at the Lime Green Delight mustache he sported, thinking, *Exactly how does one dress for a celebrity canine funeral?* And of course we all felt terrible for our childhood friend. A honeymoon, in light of this tragic development, was simply out of the question. Myrtle Beach would have to wait. And darn it, it was biker week. Of all the ways to ruin a wedding and really get to know your in-laws . . .

I have thought about that occasion often over the years. I can only assume that it's because that wedding and Tiny's untimely death were my first real (and ridiculous) introduction to the world outside the one I expected to live in when I stepped out from my structured upbringing. I expected a Norman Rockwell world, the world found in *BRIDE* magazine, the life governed by Emily Post, the universe that my mother had lived in and in which she had taught me to behave. What I got was that wedding in Columbia, Tennessee, and I will never forget it. It was Lesson No. 1 in a life full of lessons about contrasts in the South.

Incidentally, my friend and her husband were married for twenty-two years. They had two beautiful children but found that, once the kids were grown, there was nothing else that they really had in common. During that time though, she did develop a passion for hunting, so it wasn't a total loss. She got herself a dog and continues to live happily in Middle Tennessee.

Elvis

Several years after the Tiny/wedding incident, my second husband and I were invited to witness the nuptials of his long-time friend Gary. Now Gary came from a very respectable Christian family, but he was one of those children who felt compelled to rebel against his parents' example. I'm not implying that Gary wasn't a Christian; I'm simply noting that he drank too much, ate too much, spent too much, talked too loudly, delighted in telling off-color jokes, and hung around with a questionable lot.

Gary stood about 5'2" and was just as wide as he was tall. He also sported a mullet, that hideous 80s coiffure combining a short '50s crew look in the front and a long, '60s Woodstook style in the back. "Business in the front and a party in the back," was how Gary described his 'do. He was always very gifted with words.

God truly does put a mate out there for everybody, and Gary was lucky enough to have found his in a strip club in downtown Atlanta. Good thing he thought to look there; otherwise, some other lucky guy would have surely snapped her up. Chiffon (honestly, that was her name) was a tiny little thing with a twangy south-Georgia accent and no inkling of how to do anything except dance. She had quite a few talents in that arena, many of which defied gravity, but she couldn't cook, clean, entertain, or ever even think about a career change. Nonetheless, Gary loved her and couldn't marry her fast enough, much to his parents' delight . . . really.

The day of the wedding came, and we were escorted

inside the church to sit on the groom's side. The gathering of people in that church reminded me of the cast of *Smokey and the Bandit*. There were leather NASCAR jackets, black tuxedo tee shirts, sequins, spandex, big hairdos, and more mullets than you could find in any trash-strewn tidewater eddy, all sitting on the bride's side of the church.

Seated on the front row of pews were Gary's parents. I'll never forget the sight of them. Dad was straight-backed and stoic with a clenched jaw, and Mom was stoned out of her mind. She looked to be under the influence of a cocktail of several mood-altering pills and some hard liquor, but of course that's only a guess. I imagine she grabbed a handful of the first thing she could find and swallowed them with a shot of whiskey just to get through the ceremony. In hindsight, I don't blame her a bit.

And there stood Gary. I could only see the top of his hair from where I sat on the third row, but I knew it was Gary, all right. I could hear him telling an offensive joke from several rows back--something about his wedding night and the sturdiness of their bed, or something equally as romantic.

And then came the moment we'd all been waiting for--the bride's entrance. And what an entrance it was! The canned wedding music stopped abruptly, and somewhere just out of sight an electric guitar screamed out "The Wedding March." Yes, that is possible. Chiffon flounced down the aisle hanging on the arm of a pierced and tattooed escort who looked to be in his mid-seventies. I couldn't be sure if he was her dad or her brother, or both. No matter. There was the beautiful bride in all her splendor. She wore a white leather micro-skirt with a neon pink garter and white patent leather go-go boots. Her generous chest was harnessed by a white tube top and sprinkled with pink and silver glitter. A delicate spray of pink and white roses was tucked into her impressive cleavage. I couldn't remember ever seeing that ensemble in *BRIDE* magazine, but at moments like that memory often fails. It was breathtaking, I'll give her that.

I didn't have much time to ponder the father/brother angle because at just about the same time as Chiffon commenced her flouncing, Gary's mother began to sob uncontrollably. It was a gut-wrenching sound, enough to bring tears to my own eyes, and I hardly knew these people.

Then, another of those unforgettable moments happened that still stands out in sharp contrast to my ideals and standards of how things *ought* to be. When Chiffon was almost to the altar, ready to take Gary's pudgy little hand in marriage, she squeaked out, "I love you, Baby," to which Gary replied in his best Elvis voice, "Well I love you too, Honey." The electric guitar wailed a few bars of "You Ain't Nothin' But a Hound Dog." I could feel the laughter welling up from that dark place inside me, and I fought valiantly to push it back down.

Gary's mother erupted into fresh waves of sobs, his father sat ever so slightly straighter, and his sister (who was also a bridesmaid) fainted right there in front of God and everybody, inches from Gary's mother. She did; I couldn't believe it. In fact, no one could. It was as if time stood still in that split second between, "What just happened?" and

"Somebody call 9-1-1!"

I said I fought valiantly to suppress my laughter. I lost the fight when someone's eighty-pound three-year-old ran up to the collapsed bridesmaid and screamed "She's dead! She's dead!" He pronounced it "DAY-ud." This declaration made Chiffon start screaming, then faint right alongside her bridesmaid. Gary's mother stopped sobbing for the first time since the beginning of the "ceremony," I think because, for a split second, she saw a glimmer of hope that Chiffon might not wake up. I half expected her to nudge Chiffon with her foot, looking for signs of life. Gary's sister was already coming to, looking around in bewilderment and embarrassment. The hefty three-year-old screamed again. He was clearly overwhelmed.

The preacher dropped his Bible, and uttering a string of expletives, selflessly pounced on the young bride and began to administer CPR. The tube top, I'm sorry to say, was not very well constructed. I heard a wild snap when the elastic gave way, and even though I knew I shouldn't look, I couldn't help myself. The preacher (himself a short, portly man) was red-faced, panting and covered in glitter. Each time he pounded on Chiffon's considerable chest, a cloud of glitter plumed up, and a gasp would run through the crowd. He was sweating and had a hot-pink ring of lipstick around his mouth from breathing into Chiffon's. Little boys giggled, young men gawked, and old men just had a faraway look and a faint smile on their faces.

One of the groomsmen took off his jacket and threw it over the bride, but the damage had already been done.

Mothers covered their children's eyes, and several guests stood on tiptoe to get a better look. The wedding photographer snapped off a few shots of the fracas, probably to keep in his own personal library. I don't think even Emily Post herself could have prescribed appropriate responses to the improprieties on that particular moment.

Another lesson learned: people are weird. They're just weird, and those rules with which I was raised? I was beginning to suspect that not everyone played by them. Little did I know that most people had never even heard of them.

The Wedding/Séance Combo

Before I share this account of yet another wedding gone awry, I feel that I must explain something additional about the "white trash" subculture, particularly with respect to Southern white trash. I will tread lightly here because respectful reverence for the dead is expected and appropriate in any culture, Southern or alien. However, lots of white-trash folks take that reverence to the extreme. In fact, they are fanatical about their "kinfolk," their "blood," whether they still walk among us or not. Some are fanatical to the point of being bizarre and unnatural, but we'll get to that in a minute.

I have often pondered this phenomenon. I mean, I love my family. I miss most of my dead relatives. I try to speak kindly and respectfully of the dead. But I call a spade a spade, and I get the difference between a family member who's still breathing and one who has gone on to the Great Beyond, never to return.

The blissful ignorance of many white trash families is that they put all their eggs in the "family" basket. It doesn't matter if your brother is a bank robber or your uncle is wanted in seven states for check forgery; family's family. And family can do no wrong. Ever.

Oh--and let me be very clear--every family has skeletons. It's just that proper Southern families, on the one hand, lock those skeletons in closets and swallow the keys. Stoic perseverance, that's one of the earmarks of a true Southern family to whom appearances matter. Whether the secret is a baby born out of wedlock or a great-aunt who isn't rowing with both oars, it's OK as long as it remains hush-hush.

White trash, on the other hand, embrace these wayward relatives. They parade them around on their shoulders, wearing their indiscretions like badges of honor, always overlooking them, rewriting them, excusing them or blaming them on others because they're family, because they're "blood." In other words, the essential pride white trash have is in the very things that make them white trash. Does that make sense? Kind of a cultural catch-22, I know, but it's true.

Family's important, make no mistake. In my family, we hold the bar high. If you don't measure up to our expectations, somebody's going to tell you. And that's OK, in my opinion; if you don't expect, you don't get. In other words, we believe that we learn our values and develop our character under the tutelage of our parents, siblings, grandparents, aunts, and uncles.

In a white trash family, your mish-mash of genes and chromosomes is all that matters. Character doesn't matter; integrity is not important. Translation: "No matter what you do, we got your back." Or, "do unto others before they get a chance to do it unto you."

Now, on to the story. A distant cousin announced her daughter's engagement several years ago. The betrothed were two young folks growing up in modest homes in somewhat culturally deficient circumstances here in the South. Their families are fundamentally decent people, but they are without question bona fide Southern white trash. I regret to say that I intentionally missed the bridal shower. I simply couldn't reconcile the "75 cent pitchers" (of beer) touted on the invitation with the spirit of the occasion. As it turns out, the pitchers made perfect sense.

The day of the wedding arrived. It was to be a "destination" wedding, a road trip, held in the North Georgia mountains in a rundown tourist trap of a town famous for its German atmosphere and beer. *(Note: Beer is to white trash what gasoline is to fire)*.

The small ceremony was held on a mountainside that very autumn. The weather is typically breathtakingly beautiful in Georgia at that time of year, and that particular day did not disappoint. The sky was crystal blue, almost painful to look at. The leaves were turning warm shades of orange and yellow, and there was a crispness to the cool mountain air that made me feel just a bit more alive, more aware.

The groom and his men awaited the blushing bride at the outdoor altar, each man wearing a poorly fitted suit and red basketball shoes. The best man was so inebriated that he could barely stand. And that's not the funny part; it just helps paint the picture. When the bridesmaids wound their way to the altar, I saw that they too were wearing basketball shoes. Hmmm. I thought that was odd, but to each his own, I always say. I did feel a tiny fluttering in the pit of my stomach, kind of a déjà vu that hinted at past weddings gone terribly wrong.

Then came the bride, bless her heart, lumbering down the aisle in an unflattering strapless satin mini-gown that made her considerable girth even more considerable. A tattoo, one of those images designed to strike fear in the hearts of enemies, peeked daintily over the top of her bodice. A giant red bow and a long red train were the cherry on top of the cake, so to speak. All she lacked was a pigskin under one arm and numbers ironed onto the back of her gown, and the ensemble would have been complete. She too sported red high-tops. "Aha," I thought. "A theme wedding."

In truth, the ceremony itself was very sweet and surprisingly uneventful. A lovely outdoor sit-down dinner awaited us next, with tables set for six to eight people and scattered among the trees. There was a serve-yourself bar with beer and wine (remember gasoline and fire?), and the tables were set with dainty little place cards.

Marc and I searched until we found our table, then began making polite conversation with the people seated near us. I leaned over to ask him whether he had noticed the one table off to the side, with place cards saving seats . . . apparently for the bride's dead relatives. "No way," he replied. "You must have imagined it." Of course, that had to be it. Still, the investigative reporter in me wouldn't be quiet until I took another look. I excused myself from our table to get a glass of wine, and I took the path that wound alongside the unoccupied table. Gingerly stepping over the best man, who had by then passed out across the path leading to the bar, I discreetly leaned over one of the chairs. Squinting to read the place card saving that seat, I saw that the card read "Paw-Paw," as plain as day. I said a quick prayer that the groom's family also called their grandfather, present and accounted for, Paw-Paw, because the one on her side of the family had been dead for several years.

My eyes widened in surprise as I less discreetly moved from seat to seat, leaning and squinting to read the place cards. "Uncle Jim." Died in 1989. "Aunt Toots." Dead. A double-whammy there, both the name and the fact that if family legend could be believed, this woman had fallen down an abandoned well in the late 1970s and had tooted her last. My head swam. My vision blurred. "Bubba." Dead. "Ruthie Ann." Dead. I half-expected to see a place card with the name "Tiny" scrawled in calligraphy, but of course I didn't. Wrong wedding. Still, that sense of déjà vu stirred again. Creepy.

I got my glass of wine; rather, I drank one and carried a second back to our table (stepping over the best man, who had rolled over to the wedding party's table and was asleep under it), and shared my puzzling discovery with Marc. He still didn't believe me, after all that research. I convinced him to make the same rounds I had just made and sure enough, I could see by the look on his face when he came back that he was now a believer.

Now, Marc is a Southerner by transplant, having been born in Ohio but moving to Georgia as a very young boy. He grew up to be a good ol' boy. Now a good ol' boy is not necessarily a redneck (sometimes, but not always), not white trash, but just a good guy who gets along well with others and has a certain air about him that makes him very approachable. What my husband sometimes lacks, however, is the discretion so crucial to a true, proper Southerner. Taking his seat he exclaimed loudly enough for surrounding guests to hear, "What the hell is wrong with these people? Everybody at that (blank, expletive, blank) table is (blanking) dead!" Then, and I found this most distressing of all, he wondered aloud whether someone had been crazy enough to pay the caterer to prepare dinners for the dear departed guests.

My husband's two daughters arrived at the event late, missing the wedding ceremony but making it just in time for dinner. They searched for the table with their place cards, but found none. Being resourceful girls, they simply sat at the table where no one else was seated. I saw this spectacle unfold in a matter of a few seconds, but of course in retrospect I remember it in slow motion, seeming more like a half hour or so. The oldest daughter sat right in Paw-Paw's lap, or at least where his lap would have been if he had not died two years earlier. The youngest sat in Ruthie Ann's. At that moment I had the same thought as my husband's. "I wonder if they ordered food for that table?" In fact I hoped so, since the taboo seemed to have been lifted by the girls sitting there first. In just a couple of minutes, the table was full with chatting friends and relatives, all of them very much alive and hungry. It was a regular family reunion, so to speak.

This would have all been just another humorous, weird story if the family matriarch hadn't seen real-life people sitting in the laps of long-departed relatives. She began screeching--that's an accurate term, *screeching*--as she ran to the table and shooed the trespassers away, righting chairs and adjusting place cards as she went. As she shooed, she took brief breaks to talk to the chairs and apologize for her living relatives' lack of manners. Tiny the

Amazing Hunting Dog would have been proud. Not really knowing what to say or how to respond to this, I opted to get another glass of wine.

The rest of the evening rather paled in comparison, although to outsiders who hadn't witnessed the entire drama it might have raised some eyebrows. As daylight gave way to twilight and then to nightfall, guests continued to consume gallons of beer and to pontificate on the day's earlier events. Everybody was drinking beer, even many of the minor children. I actually watched a mother sling back a couple of brews while she waited for little Junior to finish nursing. I have learned over the years that the ability to consume lethal amounts of beer is sort of a white trash "coming of age" threshold, much like a Jewish bar mitzvah or a Catholic first communion. It's a proud moment along the way to puberty when your child can go toe-to-toe with you and a case of Pabst Blue Ribbon beer.

The wedding guests, those still standing anyway, were divided pretty much half and half in their opinions about the otherworldly-guest table and ordering food for dead people. One faction expressed their disbelief that the girls could show such disrespect for the dear departed. The other half expressed utter disbelief at the craziness of the whole concept. Setting a table for dead relatives? Paying $28.00 a head for their meals? But I couldn't stay focused on that issue. My mind was wandering elsewhere, specifically toward the equally vexing issue of wedding cakes. Did I mention that the groom's cake was just a stack of Little Debbie snack cakes still in their wrappers? Not only was I still wrestling with the protocol for dining with dead wedding guests, I also had to worry about whether it was proper to eat pre-packaged cake with my fingers or with a fork.

No matter. As we came to realize that evening, the "inclusion of deceased family members in family get-togethers" issue will likely never be settled among the family members. It's still debated to this day, usually over cases of beer, and Cheez-Whiz and crackers.

Yet another lesson learned: Just when you think you've seen it all, you're amazed to learn that you haven't. You really haven't.

Funerals

Funerals are just as deserving of an introduction as weddings, I suppose. Death and its subsequent rituals make me uneasy, but I doubt that I'm alone in that. Not many of us are comfortable facing the death of a loved one. It makes us shake hands with the fact that our own exit will be staring us down sooner or later.

We can't avoid the fact that a death is an important family occurrence. Whether the deceased is a close relative, a family friend, or just an acquaintance, that person was somebody's mom or dad, brother or sister, and that means that a grieving family must say goodbye.

I may have already mentioned this, but most of my family are not emotionally demonstrative people. We were taught from a very young age to hold our emotions in check, especially when in public. To lose control of our emotions, however briefly or for whatever reason, is considered unseemly, considered gauche and in poor taste. My mother's interpretation, quite simply: "White trash." I have translated that in my adulthood to mean that control of my emotions reflects a dignified reserve, a graceful calm. It stands to reason, then, that someone prone to emotional outbursts and public displays of emotion is undignified, perhaps under the influence of a mood-altering substance but, quite certainly, white trash. Some perceive my reservation as indifference or coldness, but those people simply do not understand the unwritten Southern code of conduct. True, we in the South may place too much weight on certain behaviors, but we're all about appearances here, not substance. Over and over, I've seen a mother emotionally groaning under the weight of loss of a husband or child but with countenance and behavior that would never betray what's screaming to get out. She is a Southern lady.

Flo's Funeral

I remember that the funerals I attended as a child were hushed, somber affairs. Not that I attended that many, mind you, but the ones I do remember were all pretty much the same--quiet, sad sobs, whispers, straight faces, and lots and lots of food.

I'm not sure whether my memories were shaped more by the regional culture or by my own familial customs, but nonetheless, I feel very strongly about exhibiting decorum and reserved dignity at funerals. Through the years, however, I have come to learn that my expectations are just that--mine--and much like weddings, funerals are often an excuse for families to lose their ever-lovin' minds.

A couple of years ago, a distant relative of my husband's passed away. Her death was not unexpected, as she had been ill for many years with lung disease. I remember that distinctly, because her husband and all five of her children would smoke in her presence while she sucked her life's breath from an oxygen tank. Still, her passing of course saddened her children and numerous family members. A pilgrimage "back home" was required; that much was clear.

We packed the requisite black attire and other clothes we thought we'd need and hit the road for the eight-hour drive. It was February, still the dead of winter but with Spring so close we imagined we could feel it. As sad as the occasion was, my husband and I were looking forward to the time together, a solemn-occasioned getaway, if you like. In fact we had bought a sexy little black sports car just a couple of days earlier, and we couldn't wait to hit the road in it. My husband was a little on edge, but he always gets that way when his family assembles as a group for any reason. It can be uncomfortable sometimes, with the bickering, arrests, court-ordered rehab and such. But who says you can't go home, right?

The first viewing of Flo's body was scheduled the night we arrived in Ohio. This aside may be unnecessary but in the interest of thoroughness, I have to take a minute here to explain the progression and order of this woman's funeral. As I had mentioned, Aunt Flo had been ill for many years. Her life was rather a sad one, being married to a raging, dilapidated alcoholic and having given birth to five children who put creative new spins on the term *white trash*. On any given day, you could count on at least one of her children to be in jail for a typical white-trash transgression--theft, prescription forgery, probation violations, D.U.I., public drunkenness, welfare fraud--the list never ends, it seems. The reason I'm sharing these facts with you is to help you understand the importance of Flo's funeral, at least to Flo. She had planned it for more than fifteen years. She planned it right down to the order that her beloved country music songs were to be played before the service. She had selected the preacher, her clothes, and the seating arrangements for immediate family. This poor woman lived for her funeral, as sadly ironic as I know that sounds. It meant everything to her. For that reason she had scheduled not one but two viewings, not to mention the service during which her body would be on display yet a third time, even though she had planned to be cremated, eventually. As we would later learn, she had several more delightful surprises in store for her final guests.

The viewings at the musty old funeral home went pretty much as I had expected. Family who hadn't seen each other in years picked right up as if time had not insinuated itself at all. Men who looked very uncomfortable in their ill-fitting suits and too-tight, pinchy dress shoes sat and talked with Marc for hours. They reminisced about forgotten childhood pranks, laughing almost sadly as conversation tapered off and they felt around for something else to say.

My husband's family, both the men and the women, who still live back home spent considerable time sizing me up in the way that extended-family members will do. Now, I'm not a betting woman, but I would have put down money early on that the family gossip had spread my sister-in-law's unflattering opinions of me pretty generally among the funeral guests. For years I have had the reputation among some in that family of being, for lack of a better word, "uppity." One particular gossiper might even have gone so far as to say that I am a bitch, though I would gladly educate her about the proper role of that term in the social structure of things, if she ever musters the integrity to say that directly to me. Any woman worth her salt who's reached my age had better know how to be a bitch when it's necessary, but that topic is for another book. As fiercely as many of his family disliked me based on frenzied gossip, I clutched my uppity reputation just as fiercely.

In my own defense, let me interject here that I do

take issue with being referred to as "uppity." I have a sense of propriety, good manners, and pride, which, up to a point, can be counted self-respect. If that defines "uppity," then I guess the shoe fits and I'll take two of them. Nonetheless, it was very difficult for this uppity bitch to sit quietly and not register my look of shock and surprise while listening to some of the stories I heard during that unforgettable weekend.

Not long after being introduced to one of my husband's distant cousins as the one who, as a kid, used to light himself on fire and run down the street screaming for help, I was introduced to another, a first cousin, who is now a city councilman, by the way, though "city" in this context is more than a little ironic. This cousin had the air of a man who had hit rock bottom some time earlier and, failing to pull himself up, found it easier to drag those around him down or make up lies to elevate himself. You know the type, I'm sure. Makes you want to move to rural Ohio, doesn't it?

He was mildly amusing, and I sat politely next to my husband while this cousin recounted one tale after another about being a victim of "the man" and about the lawsuits he had filed against companies who had wronged him over the years. He was, in his view, very close to a windfall litigation victory, after which all of his problems would be put to rest. He had been saying that for many years, according to my husband. And that's when this cousin started talking about his near-miss employment opportunity at Area 51 in Nevada (pronounced Nuh-VAY-duh, according to our orator).

He had come very near, it seems, to securing a top-secret position there with the government, but there had been some sort of a snag in his security clearance. As he continued to talk, I looked around at the group of people who were also listening. They were enthralled, absorbed in the tale, fascinated at the prospect of one of their blood relatives landing such a prestigious job. My eyebrows were raised, and I'm pretty sure my eyes were bugged out. It's a bad habit I've developed in place of saying something inappropriate like, "What the hell?"

I stole a quick glance at my husband, whose eyes had glazed over in that expression I know all too well. It's like, *if I just sit here and don't blink, the talking will eventually stop.* I get that expression from him a lot; I am quite familiar with it.

The security snag that this cousin had run into out in Nevada apparently had to do with a metal plate that had been surgically installed in his head following a drug deal gone bad. It seems this cousin had gotten his brains bashed in by a disgruntled drug dealer a couple of years earlier, and a sizable piece of metal now sits where most of his skull had been. Apparently it also occupies much of the space where he formerly had gray matter, but I only base that inference on this one conversation.

The plate, as it turns out, interfered with radio transmissions from outer space, transmissions that he and some government "high-ups" believed were coming from aliens trying to rescue their fallen comrades. As a result, employment at Area 51 was a no-go. And he was *so* close.

There it was again, the laughter that surges up from

that dark place inside me. I didn't even have time to check it. It just came out. I was laughing out loud, thinking that had to be the goofiest story I've ever heard, but as I looked around at the others who were privy to the conversation, they were just shaking their heads and saying things like, "Man, that's too bad" or "Don't let it get you down. You'll get your break someday." At the same time, they were looking at me like I was an uppity, heartless bitch to laugh at such a sad story, such an unlucky break.

My laughter quickly subsided, helped along by the pleading look of *please don't* I got from my husband, and I left the room to get a cup of coffee.

On the day of the funeral, we arrived a respectable fifteen minutes before the service and took our seats about halfway back, a good ten rows from the rented coffin. The ceremony was to begin at 11:00 a.m. When 11:15 came and went, then 11:30, we looked around to see what was going on. I had been staring at the tattoo and thong cheek floss of the young woman seated in front of me for quite long enough. I was ready to get this thing over with.

A whispered explanation began passing through the crowd of seated guests, and when it came to us I could hardly believe my ears. The ceremony hadn't started yet because neither the dead woman's husband nor the preacher was present. A search party had apparently been dispatched shortly after 11:00, and the two had been found together a couple of blocks down the street in a bar, drinking. They were in no shape to come to the funeral home.

I was still working on processing this latest

development when a chubby little rosy-faced man took his position behind the podium and began to deliver Flo's long-awaited eulogy. I think he must have been the new guy at the funeral home who drew the short straw, but that's just a guess.

He valiantly dove right in, talking over the strains of Conway Twitty and Merle Haggard, extolling the virtues of this kind little woman whose soul had left earth for a better place. During the eulogy, the round little man kept addressing Flo's brother as her husband. The hits just kept on coming. I did not laugh, at least not on the outside. I do recognize that that would have been improper. Flo would have turned over in her grave, had she been in it, which she was not, not yet.

When the funeral service was over, my husband and I both breathed a sigh of relief. Finally. One more required appearance at a nephew's house for the after-party, then we could go back home to sanity and our own, by then, much-more-appreciated suburban reality.

We grabbed our coats and were inching out the door when the funeral director handed us one of those little flags you put on your car antenna for a funeral procession. I thought to myself, *To where would we all process? She's being cremated. Has someone booked a bar for the occasion?* But we obediently placed the flag on the antenna, climbed into our car and waited our turn to pull out of the parking lot. Everyone else seemed to know where we were going, so we just followed along, chalking this delay up to a "wouldn't you know it" kind of experience. I watched in disbelief as the carload of funeral-goers in front of us flipped the bird at oncoming drivers who did not pull over to let the procession pass. This day just kept getting better and better. I braced myself, sure that someone ahead of us would get the bright idea to moon oncoming traffic. If that got started, the festivities wouldn't end until someone went to jail.

A few miles down the road, the parade of cars turned left into a cemetery. We thought that was odd, but, oh well. Maybe this was an Ohio burial custom, we mused. We had made it this far; what difference could another few minutes possibly make?

The procession wound around past grave sites, crypts, and memorial plaques and came to stop in front of a small square building. People filed from their cars into the building under the discreet guidance of the chubby little man and a taller, younger gentleman that I recognized from the funeral home.

People squeezed and jostled in an attempt to fit into the close quarters, but eventually we all found a spot and awaited the next act of this amusingly macabre little play. I remember glancing over at Cousin Human Torch (or should I say, "Councilman" Torch), noting that he had stopped at a gas station for a Big-Gulp. He was drinking it and staring back at me, as if marking me for his next incendiary experiment. Looking back, I remember thanking God many times for the spot by the door that we had staked out and secured.

Once everyone had squeezed into the tiny room, the tall young man began to explain that Flo's wishes were that all of her loved ones be with her during the cremation. He asked if we were ready, then reached up and pushed a button that dinged, much like a microwave timer. We heard . . . rocket engines? Jet airplanes flying overhead? By the time we both figured out that the sound we were hearing was a furnace firing up, a sweet little old lady began passing out cups of coffee, apple cider, or hot chocolate, whichever we preferred. Each Styrofoam cup featured a photo of Flo, her "start" and "stop" dates, and an ad for the Funeral Home. Is it me, or is that both opportunistic and ghoulish? Several women in the room began to cry softly and dab at their eyes with lace hankies. Human Torch sucked loudly on his straw, making that irritating slurping sound that signals the drink is all gone. No, please stop. It's all gone. Really.

Everyone else just looked around uncomfortably, like they were standing in an elevator powered by a very loud engine. I kept waiting for cameramen to pop out of a closet and yell that we were all unwitting participants in some dark and twisted version of *Candid Camera,* but they never came.

My husband and I looked at each other and, without saying a word, pushed our way out of that claustrophobic, Twilight Zone set and bolted for the car. No "goodbye," no "wow, that was weird." Nothing.

For the record, when we were safely in the car with the doors locked, we both convulsed in laughter, not just me. To this day I'm not sure whether that laughter was born of hilarity or horror. I suppose it doesn't matter, does it?

As tempted as we were to point the car southeast and just start driving, we came to our senses when we reached our hotel. The after-party (or wake or whatever you want to call it) still loomed before us, and it would have been rude to skip out without saying our goodbyes. Truthfully, I was way past worrying about being rude to Human Torch or Area 51 or most of the others, but my husband would have regretted it if we had bugged out like that. We decided to stay a bit longer, make an appearance, make an excuse, then leave.

The town in which my husband's family lives in Ohio is very small, built around an old town square that is the center of the community. Nearly all the houses in the town look pretty much alike. Don't get me wrong; there's nothing wrong with that. In fact, it made me think that it might be kind of nice to live in a place where there didn't appear to be any "haves" and "have-nots." Pretty much everyone's circumstances in the community appeared closer to the condition of have-not than have, but if you can't make the distinction is anyone really a have-not? I don't think so.

The directions we were given for the location of the after-party went something like this: "Go up yonder 'til you see the courthouse, then turn around lookin' away from the courthouse and you'll see a gas station. Then look up. That big house on the hill is Junior's house. That's where it is."

We had been hearing about Junior's house all weekend. It was fabulous, stupendous, huge and very fancy, according to the accounts we were getting from the relatives. Now, I'm going to pause a minute here to examine another white-trash trait, and that's the tendency to embellish when it comes to bragging about one of your relatives. I've had a lot of time to think about this, so hear me out.

First, remember that white-trash family is tight, no matter what. And remember also that the bigger the loser, the more proud he makes his family. Those facts, soaked in beer, result in some odd accounts that pit reality against fantasy in somewhat awkward situations. For example, one time I was being shown a yellow-gold watch that an acquaintance's girlfriend had given him for Christmas. At the same time I was examining the watch, his parents were telling me that it was a solid-gold timepiece, a very extravagant gift for such a young relationship. "She comes from money, and I mean a lot of it," was the exact quote from his mom, I believe. The whole time I'm politely listening to the story, I'm holding the watch and reading "T-I-M-E-X" in plain black-and-white print on the face of it. Of course, I didn't say anything, but later I told my husband that that must be one of the watches that Wal-Mart keeps under lock and key, the solid gold Timexes. It only makes sense.

Anyway, the big fine house that I saw while facing away from the courthouse and looking just over the gas station was a dilapidated double-wide trailer. It was perched precariously on the side of a hill and sported an added-on front porch and a separate carport in the yard, like the ones you can order from Sears & Roebuck.

That couldn't be right. I turned again to face the courthouse, turned away again, spotted the gas station, and looked up. There it was again in all its glory, Junior's big fine house. In fact, it had to be. That was Junior's motorcycle parked on the front porch, and I recognized several funeral guests on that same porch drinking out of bottles, each wrapped in a paper bag. Yes, that had to be the place.

Please don't misunderstand. There is absolutely nothing wrong with having few material possessions and a modest home. This demographic makes up the heart of America. I grew up in a modest home, raised by parents who lived through the Great Depression. I am not a material snob. What I do have a problem with is people exaggerating or just plain lying. Whatever your circumstances in life, own them. Don't paint them loud colors to try to make them look like something they're not. In my opinion, that just makes you look foolish and fraudulent. But I digress.

My husband and I looked at each other, then back at Junior's palace, and breathed a deep sigh. We had come this far, so why not? I mean, how much worse could it possibly get?

I shouldn't have asked.

I'll be brief here, just try to give you a feel for what happened over the next hour or so.

There was a line forming in the "living room" for relatives who wanted memorial tattoos. Someone had apparently sprung for an on-site ink artist.

Two mangy dogs were helping themselves to a stack of bologna sandwiches on a tray on the kitchen table, sharing their find with a filthy little kid dressed only in a diaper and sitting on a used paper plate.

A child no more than three or four years old was

delivering two canned beers to a couple on the velvet sofa. He presented the beverages by naming their brands--and opening them.

Flo's older brother sat alone in a corner wondering aloud why on earth the stand-in preacher (not all that familiar with the family) would refer to him as his own sister's husband. I'm guessing he didn't hear the aforementioned whispered comments of explanation for the delay in the services, about the missing husband/preacher/bar thing. I didn't have the heart to tell him that his toupee had slipped down over one ear.

When we left the palace that evening, my husband vowed we'd never return to Ohio for any reason, ever. Of course as it turns out he was wrong, but that story will come later.

The "Pass the Cup" Funeral

Before I launch into this funeral story, I'm going to pause to dissect and explain another white-trash phenomenon. This sidebar will help shed light on the events, so bear with me.

In the white-trash world, money and the lack of it set the tone for pretty much every family function, even funerals. Now a respectable white-trash family will always have money for beer, cigarettes, cable TV, and NASCAR memorabilia, but when it comes time to pony up for a big expense (such as a funeral), the poor-mouthing begins. Another side note: Those in the family known for excessive drinking, drug binges, or a penchant for getting arrested will launch into poor-mouthing during any such times of family crisis. It's just human nature to play to our strengths during times of stress.

Poor-mouthing, you ask? That's the practiced art of proclaiming to everyone within earshot how poor you are. How *broke* you are, to use the proper terminology. Poor-mouthing is usually put into play for one of two reasons. First, it can serve as a form of trolling; if you spread the word far and wide enough that you have no money, odds are someone will give you some just to shut you up. Eventually, it becomes habit, an expectation, a knee-jerk reaction. Second, if you poor-mouth long and loud enough when a big family expense crops up (like a funeral), relatives are less likely to expect you to contribute financially. You see, white-trash families do not waste money on savings accounts, life insurance, or burial policies. It simply isn't done. I think that grieving for the RECENTLY DEPARTED WHITE TRASH LOVED ONE is partially alleviated by the mad scramble to avoid getting stuck with part or all of the bill. Now that we are up to speed, I can go on with this particular account of a recent family funeral.

About a year ago, a close relative of my husband's passed away. Let's call him Bubba. Again, death was not a surprise; years of drinking, smoking, and unchecked diabetes had racked his body and left him extremely frail. He probably would have passed much sooner than he did, but his frequent stints in various county jails helped him regulate his insulin much better than he would have if left to his own devices. Sad, but very true.

Now Bubba was the poster child for poor white trash. He was irresponsible, unaccountable, and had no qualms about stealing from family, friends, and strangers. It was just his way, and everyone who knew him expected nothing more from him. It came as no surprise, then, that when he died he left various debts and all of his funeral arrangements and expenses to those he left behind. Bubba's son and his son's common-law wife stepped in when his father became very ill, taking over his disability checks and the rest of his unfinished business. When it became apparent that death was imminent, we received a visit from these two, and the chatter began--the "dance," as I have come to call it: remarks like, "He doesn't have enough money to pay his bills, let alone pay for a funeral, and we just don't have it." And so on.

And on.

And on.

The picture was coming clear, and my husband and I had anticipated this visit all along. We had been through this "dance," the "My funeral is your problem" fox trot. All the tell-tale signs were there. Poor-mouthing, pregnant pauses, more poor-mouthing, expectant stares. You get the idea.

Among many of my husband's relatives, we are considered wealthy. Nothing could be further from the truth, but everything is, well, relative, isn't it? Perception is reality; so, when it comes time to scratch for bail money, funeral money, or any other money that someone else in the "family" just didn't feel like working for, we are among those to receive the trolling phone call, early on. In the land of white trash, any family member who makes good, who actually earns a living without sponging off others and the government, owes his family an equal level of comfort. It's an entitlement thing that ties back to the blood-is-thicker-than-water thing. Are you still with me? With the understanding that money brings out the absolute worst in people, let's unravel this little anecdote.

Now my husband and I knew exactly what was expected once the initial "We don't have the money" visit took place, but for once we didn't take the bait. Still raising our own children, we had decided to make the last funeral we helped pay for, well, the last (at least for a while, God willing).

Of course, the day came when Bubba finally died. The weeks of family pilgrimages, hand wringing and hopeful ups and downs were over. It was a cold rainy day in early Spring. I remember that because I was surprised to see a woman standing in my driveway when I came home that blustery morning; she looked very "out of context" to me. She was pacing back and forth in the driveway and smoking a cigarette--in the rain. It was the common-law wife, and she had apparently spun herself into a frenzy while she paced and smoked.

I had no sooner turned off the ignition and opened my car door when she pounced. "We figure your part is about a thousand dollars," she said. In my driveway, at my house, before I could even get inside, she was panhandling. A dark sense of déjà vu began to stir.

I walked inside to see family members draped all over the living room furniture; they had made a beeline from the hospital to our house. Not a good sign. No one was saying much really, except for the wet smoker. The air of expectation was palpable; the figurative hand was out. I walked right through the room, stepping over "broke" mourners, went into my office and closed the door. I knew that that solution was too simple, and my suspicions were confirmed when the wet smoker followed me into my office, shut the door and began to vent. There's an art to this dance--vent about other people shirking their responsibilities, and that translates into "be prepared to pick up the slack." As I said, this wasn't my first fox trot.

Eventually the mourning party left, all of them wearing puzzled looks as they filed out the door. Unaccountably, in their view, they were leaving without a check, cash, money order, or merchandise, a phenomenon they had never experienced before when leaving our house.

Their world had tilted on its axis; this was a new reality none of them had ever fathomed. Usually, when white trash lays enough guilt on a relative who has pulled himself up by his bootstraps, there is always a payoff. But not on that day. The First National Bank of Townsend was not open for business. This monumental occurrence--no money changing hands--would have a ripple effect over the next couple of days, the likes of which would make any white-trash dynasty proud. Without dragging the tale out longer than is necessary, here's a brief summary of the events that followed.

My husband's sister and brother-in-law, who probably really couldn't afford to chip in for funeral expenses, took out a loan for the entire amount required to display and cremate the deceased. This makes no sense, I know, but there is very little money management savvy in the white-trash world. Emotions often decide how money is spent, and how it's borrowed.

The nephew and his common-law wife, who should have shouldered the entire expense if the tales about his windfall inheritance and her insurance fraud scheme were to be believed, bailed and paid nothing. Now these tales may have been of the same variety as the solid gold Timex (remember Junior's palace and the solid gold watch?), but who knows? According to the aforementioned borrowers, the nephew had promised to pay but later denied making any such promise.

As a result, the sister and brother-in-law filed a lawsuit against Bubba's son and common-law wife. This wasn't all bad, as the lawsuit gave the sister a completely new topic about which to gossip.

The memorial service took place before a packed house there to witness a very positive spin placed on a misspent life fraught with petty crime, irresponsibility, and countless scams and arrests. No siblings, aunts, uncles, or cousins present spoke to one another before, during, or after the ceremony, as everyone was mad about something. In contrast, everyone there had the highest praise and admiration for Bubba, who had screwed (literally or figuratively) each and every person in the room at one point in his life. All of his ex-wives and children and creditors were there, crying and bemoaning their loss. And I was in the rabbit hole once again, at a complete loss as to how to explain this upside-down spectacle. I was dumbfounded.

My husband and I stuck to our guns, though, turning the tables on the usual "receivers" in the family. For a change, someone else was out thousands of dollars that they'll surely never see again. Blood truly is thicker than water, but cash trumps blood any day. Another happy ending.

The Family Jewel

Back in the late 1990s, when I was at the peak of my marketing career, raising two young children, and pretty much getting my bearings as a self-sufficient woman, I got the sad news that a long-ago friend of mine had passed away quite unexpectedly. He and I had dated briefly when I was a young, impressionable teen. I had met this young man while visiting my cousin on her family's farm in Alabama, and I immediately fell head-over-heels for him. Of course I did; he was everything my mother would have disapproved of on every conceivable level. His family was not just white trash but *poor* white trash. He was uneducated, having dropped out of high school in the tenth grade to help his daddy work the family farm. But he was big and muscular, tan, impossibly good-looking, and I was hooked.

The relationship lasted barely the summer. When I returned to the urban and urbane world of Atlanta, Mike became a faint but fond memory.

I was very surprised, years later, to hear from my cousin that Mike had just been killed in a car accident. He couldn't have been older than forty. For some reason death is always a little sadder, a little harder to understand, when it comes too soon. I'm still not sure why I felt compelled to attend the funeral, but I did. I made arrangements to meet my cousin in the small town of Eufaula, Alabama, where the service was to be held. It was September, still very hot and muggy here in the deep south.

Visitation, which I believe we defined before as the

period during which family and friends can gather and ogle the body before it's buried or cremated, was held on Friday evening.

Let me stop a second here and ask, is it just me, or have you ever witnessed how some people feel compelled to poke and stroke a dead body while it's lying there prone in the casket? I think it's a gruesome and bizarre practice, but it's pretty much universal. Did we do that when the person was alive? Just walk up to him and poke him on the cheek or pinch his hand? I never did, anyway.

In fact, when the funeral is a back-country affair, it's not unusual to see people stroke, poke, and kiss the body, throwing in a wail or a shriek for good measure. When you're white trash, the louder you wail at a funeral, the more you loved the deceased. The worse you treated him or her in life, the louder you wail. It's kind of like penance. Maybe that's just my take on things, but I've seen it enough to be convinced. I brace myself at these funerals, expecting to see a loved one actually climb into the casket with the dead body and spoon with it. Decorum and reservation are not important to the seedy sub-culture we know as white trash.

My cousin and I arrived at the funeral home promptly at 7 p.m. We planned to stay an hour or so, then have dinner at the hotel restaurant to catch up with each other. It had been years, requiring a lot of catching up!

About twenty or so minutes into the "visitation" portion of the festivities, my cousin suggested we walk up to the casket and pay our respects by looking at the body. It's at this time that one is expected to say things like, "My, my. He looks so natural" or, "My, my. He looks so peaceful." No he doesn't. He looks gray and stiff and heavily-made-up. This is another custom I'll never understand, but never mind. My cousin and I politely joined the short line to wait our turn.

Over the hushed tones of guests in Mike's "holding" room, I thought I could hear voices coming from one of the anterooms. They were whispers, but the voices were loud enough to be heard through closed doors. I asked my cousin if she heard what I was hearing, and after a minute she said yes, she did. Always a lover of gossip or even just a juicy tale, she suggested we be quiet and try to understand what was being said. The voices sounded strained and angry, almost to the point of hysteria.

"He meant for me to have it. He said so the last time I saw him."

"He never would have said that. Ever since I told him I'm gonna have his baby, he said it was mine! It had a special meaning to both of us."

"We'll see about that. Me and his mama have talked about this before. You'll take it off him over my dead body!"

Our eyes widened both in surprise and (I'm embarrassed to say) delight. We looked at each other as if to ask, "Could we really be so lucky? Gossip like this at a time like this?" We wondered silently who on earth was arguing, and what on earth they could possibly be arguing about. It wasn't long before both questions were answered.

A dark paneled door just to the right of the casket flew open, and two very angry young women tumbled out, almost tripping over each other in a race to get to the casket first. One was tall, thin and wiry, overly-tanned and with a look about her that hinted of missing teeth and inbreeding. Her hair was white-blonde, straight out of a bottle. The other woman was shorter and very pregnant.

No wait, they weren't making their way to the casket; they were heading for Mike's mother, a leathery, muscular woman who had seen her share of hard work and heartache over the years. Her son's passing was just one in a long line of trials, judging by the wear that showed on her face. At the stormy approach of the two younger women, her look of sadness was immediately replaced by a look of anger and impatience, an expression she had apparently worn often in her life because it looked very natural on her.

Both young women reached her at the same time, and both started talking, then yelling, over each other. We couldn't make much sense of what they were saying for a moment. Then the pregnant woman spoke up and said that she intended to take Mike's belt buckle home with her when she left that evening. It had sentimental value, and she meant for her baby to have it one day.

Did I hear that right? His belt buckle? My cousin and I looked at each other, eyes wide and eyebrows raised, then nonchalantly sauntered closer to where the drama was unfolding. As we drew closer, we learned a few things. So did everyone else in the entire funeral home, not just in Mike's parlor. It seems that Skinny-and-Blonde was Mike's current wife. The two were estranged, but only because woman #2 had entered the picture (apparently about seven months earlier from the looks of things, give or take).

These two were actually arguing over the belt buckle that my dead friend was wearing! Sadly, I was unable to resist pursuit of the obvious question: What on earth was so special about this belt buckle? Was it made of platinum? If so, I was throwing my hat in the ring. Otherwise, well, nothing else made sense.

My cousin was completely engrossed in the conversation by this point. My curiosity was killing me, so I headed off in the direction of the casket, committing the ultimate funeral faux pas of breaking in line ahead of everyone else waiting to poke and pat the deceased. So focused was I on getting a good look at the belt buckle that I actually leaned into the casket to get the best possible vantage point. That was a mistake.

Hearing a commotion behind me, I turned around in time to see both young women running toward me while taking intermittent jabs and punches at the other. I don't know much about brawling, but I know a thing or two about self-preservation. I quickly sidestepped the oncoming catfight, just in time for both women to crash into the casket. I cringe just recalling the next couple of minutes, even though I am writing this almost twelve years after it happened. Yes, this happened.

Skinny-and-Blonde hit the casket first, having been shoved hard enough by incipient-baby's mama to land practically right on top of poor Mike. While she was scrambling to free herself from the confines of Mike's near-final resting place, she tipped the casket just enough to upset it. It teetered precariously on the edge of the platform, then unceremoniously spilled Mike halfway out onto the flower-stand-laden floor.

Oddly, at this point, you could have heard a pin drop, literally. Not a gasp, not a wail, not a sound. A hushed blanket of shock covered all the mourners, save two. The two women paused long enough for Skinny-and-Blonde to get back onto her feet, and they went at it again. Their hands were twisted around handfuls of each other's hair. Pantyhose were ripped and torn, and skirts were hiked up leaving nothing to the imagination. Canned organ music continued to play softly as a backdrop to the fracas. The whole scene was grotesquely fascinating.

Strangely enough, it took several minutes for anyone even to attempt to break it up. Mike's mother stood just far enough away from the women to avoid getting clocked. She yelled at both of them to remember where they were and to "get ahold of yourselves," but of course that didn't help. Both women were possessed; they had gone over the edge. I don't know if you've ever seen white-trash women brawl, but there comes a point at which you just have to let them wind down on their own. To step in and to interfere would be not only useless but downright self-destructive.

I think that of all the priceless images I remember from that evening, the moment at which both women were clutching at Mike's pants trying to wrench the belt buckle free is the one that will stick in my mind forever. I couldn't help myself. I had to see it, and then it was as if God himself had heard me and decided to grant me that wish. I saw that the women had wrenched the buckle free of the belt and the belt free of Mike's pants. I won't go into everything that was revealed that evening, but I saw the silver buckle winking and glinting from between the sweaty hands trying to lay claim to it. It slipped, or rather shot, out of their hands and flew skyward, turning and twirling as if in slow motion as everyone stared at it, mouths hanging open and eyes wide.

The buckle came to rest at my feet. I looked down, blinked and bent to pick it up, even though I knew on some level that my move might be very dangerous.

I turned the treasure over in my hands, eager to see and appreciate the value of such a coveted artifact. The buckle itself was silver, big, and gaudy . . . and big, really big. It had the words "Dollywood," inscribed in large raised letters on the front, and "Pigeon Forge, Tennessee" etched on the back. The buckle also doubled as a bottle opener. How ingenious, and how handy! No wonder they both wanted it!

In the background, George Jones overtook the organ music and crooned something about a deceivin' woman beatin' his poor heart to death. I looked from my long-ago friend Mike to his wife, to his girlfriend, to my cousin. The belt buckle slid from my hand onto the floor, cushioned by the thick rug of flower petals that now carpeted nearly the entire room. I'm not much of a beer drinker, but all of a sudden I had an unquenchable thirst for one . . . at least.

"Let's get out of here," I mumbled to my cousin. My mother's doubts about Mike all those years ago were right. Damn it.

In the Nick of Time

A few years back my husband, Marc, and I went through a period during which one of his relatives passed away about every four or five months. I suppose every family has a season like that, and it's hard, emotionally grueling. Someone told me one time that if you want to see what people are made of squeeze them really hard. They're made of what comes out. I'd have to say I agree with that observation.

About five years after Marc and I married, his father passed away. We were very sad, of course. There's always unfinished business it seems, when a parent dies. I tried my best to be the wife that my husband needed me to be, both supportive and consoling, grieving but strong.

There's a mechanism that kicks in when death takes someone we love. The business of tying up the loose ends of someone else's life, I think, is the very thing that keeps us from being overwhelmed by the grief in the days following a death. I have seen wives and mothers, grief-stricken husbands and children busy themselves during the week or so following a loved one's death. During that time when you'd think those people would be devastated beyond their ability to function, they perform heroically. It's when the business of a life is done, after all the guests have left, that grief gets a tight grip and threatens to slowly strangle.

While I certainly do not mean to imply that white-trash families do not know the same debilitating grief that we all feel at such a sad time, I will say that they have their own knack for distracting themselves just enough to help them get through it. You'll recall what I mentioned earlier about it being human nature to play to our strengths during times of crisis. A death is no exception.

There are people (and maybe you know one or two) who tend to "act out" at the very times that they need to be doing anything but. Those people will be sure to get locked up, pokied, arrested right before, let's say, Christmas. There are those who will overindulge in alcohol, or whatever, at Thanksgiving. Easter? Punch out your wife, wreck your car. The Fourth of July? I don't even want to think about it. Intentionally or not, they seem to time their indiscretions to coincide with family-oriented holidays. More bang for the buck, so to speak.

When Marc's father, God rest his soul, passed away, the stars were in alignment for an event of epic proportions. Not only did he die; he did it right after Thanksgiving. The scene was set for a memorable hoe-down, and tradition was not disappointed.

My husband's family began making the pilgrimage down South as soon as they heard the sad news. Some flew, some drove, but everyone who intended to come did so immediately. Let me insert an observation here; maybe you can relate. Every family has members who try to turn any gathering into a fun family reunion, a party. I am not of the opinion that the death of a loved one is a great excuse for "party." I believe the focus of the gathering should be on the life and accomplishments of the deceased and on support of the grieving family. In the case of many white-trash families, however, the great potential impediment to this noble theory is that alcohol will without a doubt be a factor. It's a given. And again, anyone in this particular family old enough to hold a beer bottle by himself will be partaking in the fluid grieving process, at least in my experience. Gasoline on a fire, I'm telling you.

The day before my father-in-law's funeral, Marc's next-older brother, Don, decided to take his older brother, Dick, out for a ride in his new car. The car, though previously owned, was new to Don. It was kind of sporty, and he was very proud of it. Never mind that Don's driver's license had been suspended about twenty years earlier and never reinstated. That didn't stop him. It never stopped him. He was a victim of the system, and cops throughout the Southeast "picked on him." Law enforcement, generally speaking, was just out to get him. No one could figure it out. He just seemed to have the worst luck when it came to legal matters. Very puzzling.

So it was that Don and Dick embarked on a short joy ride on the eve of my father-in-law's funeral--innocent enough, just two guys out testing the limits of a fun little car. They went zipping down Highway 11 in South Carolina, a two-lane speed-trap nightmare of a country road, at a rate considerably above the clearly posted limit.

Inevitably, the blue lights with which Don was intimately familiar appeared in his rearview mirror. Of course, when the officer came to the window to talk to him, the first thing that came out of Don's mouth was a lie. He said that Dick was driving. Now, the steering wheel was on Don's side, but in his mind that was a perfectly plausible lie. Do you think the officer bought it? Exactly. Don was led away in handcuffs, leaving Dick to get the car back to his mother's house, and, of course, to break the news to the family that, once again, bail money was required in a time of crisis. Pass the hat, and pronto.

The arrest was not for speeding, by the way. It was for the countless minor transgressions that Don would never bother to clear up. They were petty, careless, stupid illegalities, and that's another thing I want to address here. None of his brushes with the law was ever for anything exciting or intriguing, like bank robbery or international money laundering. They were for stupid things, like not showing up in court or not paying fines or not bothering to reinstate a legal license. When this man hit the jail system, as he did quite frequently, he got passed around from jurisdiction to jurisdiction like a juicy rumor. His accrual speed for fines and penalties matched that of the national debt, and he never paid a single one of them himself. It was the family's obligation, the family's burden. And when I say "family," I mean the ones who weren't "broke." Everyone else was "broke" all the time. It's that "blood-is-thicker-than-water" thing, and it's that "let's accommodate the ones who prefer not to work" thing. No one ever addressed the real problem, which is that a member of the family was so irresponsible, or dumb, or whatever you want to call it, that he couldn't seem to stay out of jail. Going to jail is to die-hard white trash what getting the oil changed is to the rest of us. It's just a fact of life, a minor but occasionally necessary irritation, something that's expected to happen.

I'm sure you can see where this is going. The family had a dilemma, a crisis layered on top of a crisis:

Dad was to be buried in less than twenty-four hours, and Don was in jail. In my mind, that's not a dilemma; it's simply a fact. It was the result of a chain of poor choices and bad decisions. Period.

Now it was my sister-in-law's turn to chime in. Her role in the family (as far back as I can recall) is to spread guilt, disharmony, and general bad ju-ju throughout the entire clan. Oh, she's harmless enough, I suppose; one could even say that her admonishments are intended for the greater good of the family. Unfortunately, the family's "greater good" typically involves our writing a check, and that check is, typically, never quite enough to right the wrong. She means well and uses her energy generously toward that end. Sadly, her efforts, more often than not, wind up spreading hostility among several families, not just within her own.

Some years ago, she appointed herself the trustee of everyone else's finances and time; no one ever gave enough of either to support "the family," and she made it her job to hammer this fact home. This slammer/funeral problem was right down her alley. I'm not sure whether we were her first phone call, but I have no doubt we were near the top of her list. Here's how it works: you begin calling for money by starting with the most fiscally sound relative, followed by the next, etc. It's a law-of-averages thing. The call commences with a demand for money and ends with a guilt trip. In this case, the guilt trip meant questioning how we could be so coldhearted as to let Don sit in jail while his dad was being buried. Thus flows the convoluted logic of, well, you know.

By the end of the day, the family had ponied up enough money to get Don out of jail just in time for the funeral and the wake-slash-keg party. Another disaster averted.

The after-party was held at my husband's parents' house. Family members sat on the porch and under shade trees, laughing as they remembered some of the hundreds of funny stories about my father-in-law. He too was a Good Ol' Boy, and many loved him. However, as I believe I have mentioned earlier, the beer started flowing immediately after the funeral. An hour or so into the family gathering, everyone twelve and older was pretty much plastered, except for our children and myself.

Uncle Joe amused himself and terrified the grandchildren by taking his teeth out and presenting them singing "My Baby Does The Hanky Panky," like a ventriloquist. The brothers sat on the front porch reminiscing about arrests, incarcerations, and various near-misses. The underage nieces and nephews played beer pong at the kitchen table. Marc's aunt snapped photos left and right, planning yet another edition of the growing family scrapbook. Ah, good times.

The Clothes Make the Man (or Woman)

I'm going to confess to something here that I don't think I've truly faced until recently. I'm what many women would call a sloppy dresser. I prefer to think of my style of dress as casual and comfortable, sometimes a little edgy, but I will say that I've become accustomed to wearing leggings, big, baggy sweatshirts, and such. I think it all stems from once being a fat kid. I've never gotten over that.

There are certain places here in the South in which women would not be caught dead dressing as I do. Thankfully, Atlanta is not one of them. This city is such a diverse, cosmopolitan melting pot, nobody really stands out anymore. But there are some Southern cities, such as Memphis and Charleston, in which a mere trip to the mailbox requires full makeup and a well put-together ensemble. It's kind of a Stepford Wives with Grits concept I know, but true nonetheless.

There are occasions for which I do dress well, weddings and funerals included. Whether the purpose is for celebration or for paying respects, even I know that leggings and sweatshirts are not appropriate. And over the years, I have managed to collect a few "good" pieces of both jewelry and clothing. I break them out whenever necessary.

Here's another confession. I love bling. I love glitz, I love glitter, and I love sparkle. While I do own several pieces of heirloom jewelry, I own a lot more cosmetic jewelry. You know, the fun stuff. I can't help it; I just love it. The bigger, the better.

Now, I know that sparkle and glitz are completely inappropriate at a funeral and at most weddings. Like wearing white before the Derby or after Labor Day is an unforgivable no-no, so are flashy accessories at certain events. Keeping this in mind, let me share with you a few accounts of experiences I've had at some of my favorite white trash events.

A few years ago, my husband and I attended his uncle's funeral. We were in Middletown, Ohio, in the dead of winter. It was a cold, dark, miserable place to be, especially to an Atlanta native. No green could be seen anywhere. Ice and dirty snow lined the streets, and a crusty film of salt covered everything.

My husband had warned me ahead of time that it would be very cold where we were going. I immediately thought to pack my "fur" coat, a faux masterpiece that I simply had to have and, yet, for which I have never had either the occasion or the climate to wear here in Atlanta.

We arrived at the funeral home right on time for the old man's proceedings. A sizable crowd was in attendance, so we quietly took our seats in the back of the room, the section typically set aside for those young families finding it necessary bring small children to such an event. Sure enough, we were surrounded by little ones and their mommies.

Let's pause for a brief review: The Southern subcultures I have identified--white trash, trailer trash, and even rednecks--sometimes blur geographic boundaries. You may find some trailer trash in Colorado. You may even find an uprooted redneck in California. And white trash abounds in Ohio.

At this funeral, my husband and I sat directly behind a young white-trash family with their soon-to-be full-fledged white-trash kids. I knew this without exchanging a single word with any of them. How, you ask?

Mom, who had long, stringy hair that hadn't been washed in more than a week, was wearing a get-up that I couldn't have dreamed up on my most creative day. Her black tank top didn't quite meet the black sequined miniskirt she wore in honor of the deceased. Her red bra straps peeked out from under the tank top. But the pièce de résistance was the sight to which we were all treated every time she leaned over to pick her son's pacifier up off the floor.

A black thong, accented with red hearts, flashed my husband and me every time Junior dropped his binky. The thong string rested on a tattoo that started somewhere below the band of the skirt and ended somewhere underneath the tank top. From what I could make out (more than I wanted), it appeared to be a full-color winged dragon, together with script written below. In truth I didn't see enough of the letters to enjoy the full effect; to have leaned over further and looked any closer would have been completely inappropriate.

In perfect complement to Mom's attire was Dad's, or the man who I'm assuming sired the little boy in Mom's lap. He too showed deference to the occasion by dressing conservatively. His sleeveless black-flannel shirt, black jean jacket, and white polyester trousers worked well with her ensemble. His mullet was neatly brushed back into a ponytail, and the tattoo that encircled his neck and ran Lord knows how far down his back was quite striking. There was absolutely no question that they were a couple. Even little Junior had the scraggly beginnings of a mullet. Because his nose hadn't been wiped in quite some time, I fought to keep from gagging every time he peeked over Mom's shoulder to play hide-and-seek with me.

When the service was over and everyone was milling about greeting friends and relatives, my husband and I were donning our coats and chatting as we made our way toward the door. I was stopped by a tug at my coat sleeve, then by a big hug from my sister-in-law Theresa, whom I hadn't seen in several months. I was very happy to see her, and the three of us found a quiet corner to sit and catch up on each other's lives.

After about fifteen minutes, our little trio had grown to about ten or twelve people. Everyone chatted quietly but excitedly, a common phenomenon at funerals. You are happy to see many of the people there, but the circumstances require a hushed tone of voice. We quickly made plans to take our little reunion to a local restaurant.

Theresa went to the front receiving room to retrieve her coat, and she came back to the expression of "oohs" and "ahhs" from the women in our little group. The fuss they were making was over the beaver coat she was wearing. It was full, thick, and looked very warm. Of course, in my opinion, it would have looked much better on the beavers from which it was taken, but I kept that thought to myself. We were smack in the middle of hunting country, and most people here hunted for the food and fur, not for sport. I didn't want to offend anyone.

Then the attention turned to my coat, but I quickly made it clear that the fur was not a collection of real pelts from some poor woodland creatures. It was manufactured. That statement drew some puzzled stares, but no matter. I deftly turned the attention back to Theresa's coat made of harvested beaver pelts.

She then embarked on telling us the story behind the coat. Her husband, Dick, Marc's brother, was an avid hunter before he died. He loved to trap, shoot, hammer, taze, or tackle anything that ran around free in the wild. He always made good and thorough use of the meat or fur he took, but still . . .

Anyway, Theresa had also developed a love for hunting during her marriage to Dick. They would go deep into the woods for days at a time to hunt whatever was in season. Apparently, hunting is one of those things that can bring a couple closer together.

It had taken him over a year, but Dick had finally accumulated enough beaver pelts to have a coat made for his wife. On the day that he took the pelts to the tailor, however, he discovered that he was one pelt shy of a full coat. Theresa was devastated. Who knew when they'd finally get that last little trusting beaver to turn over his hide to them? Hunting season was about over, and neither Theresa nor Dick had the stomach for another full-scale assault.

Weeks passed, and no beaver pelt. Of course, Theresa was more driven than her husband to get that last one. A woman motivated by fur knows no limits. One cold and rainy afternoon, as Theresa drove home from work, she spotted a dark lump on the side of the road. At first, she couldn't tell whether it was an animal or a bag of trash. As she got closer, however, she saw that not only was it an animal; it was a beaver! Now I never would have made the leap in my mind that Theresa did, but I've never been mouthwateringly close to having a full-length beaver coat, either.

Without hesitation, Theresa whipped her Chevy over into the breakdown lane on the highway. She stepped out into the cold rain (which had turned to sleet at this point), popped her trunk open, and ran around to the soaked and frozen carcass on the ground. She reached down, took hold of the flat tail that had, in the creature's former life, warned other beavers of danger, and pried the carcass off the frozen shoulder. When I think of the sound that must have made, I get a little. . . . Right now I'm a little. . . .

Then she threw the thing in her trunk, slammed the lid, wiped her hands on her pants, and drove happily home with the prize she'd been coveting--that one last beaver.

Long story short, Theresa is now the proud owner of a genuine beaver coat. She'll never hear it from me, but if you look very closely, I think you can see tire tracks on the lower-right front panel of the coat. That knowledge would just break her little heart.

Holidays

The real tapestry of any family is woven not just of its weddings or its funerals but in the year-in, year-out gatherings we all enjoy. In this category I include holidays, birthdays, graduations, family reunions and other festivities. These festivities are wrapped in tradition, warmth, and love, and they are the stuff of which memories are made.

The same is true for white-trash families; it's just that their festivities are always so much more eventful and colorful than the rest of ours. Often domestic violence, drug overdoses, arrests, and trips to the emergency room go hand-in-hand with the warmth and love. They are, in fact, part of the tradition.

I believe I mentioned earlier that I have a tendency to "Norman Rockwell-ize" family events, and I'm particularly guilty of this on holidays. For instance, I always look forward to Thanksgiving and Christmas as times of family happiness and closeness. I try to prepare perfect, traditional meals. I try to get just the right present for each person, and I try to instill in my children traditions that they'll carry on to their families, and so on, and so on.

So I must take some responsibility for the fact that holidays never go as I imagine they should.

Thanksgiving

Take, for instance, Thanksgiving. Like so many people, including you perhaps, I grew up in a family in which Thanksgiving was a huge gathering of family and an almost indecent profusion of food. The Thanksgiving meal itself was almost a religious experience, and everyone understood several cardinal rules that applied as a result.

(1) We were absolutely never, under any circumstances, to be late for the meal. To arrive late or even worse, to not show up at all, would show great disrespect to the cooks (of which there were many). Again respect is communicated through good manners.

(2) We were always expected to dress for the occasion. To neglect this expectation would again demonstrate disrespect to the cooks and, I suppose, our forefathers. I'm not talking about black-tie dinners, but we all dressed in what those of us here in the South refer to as our "Sunday best."

And (3) while at the table (whether for the Thanksgiving meal or for any other), proper manners were of utmost importance. Some of the worst injuries I sustained as a kid were at the hands of my mother and administered at the dinner table. Chewing with your mouth open? You'd get a fork in your side. Elbows on the table? A fork in the elbow. My mother wielded her utensils like "nunchucks". Her immune system must have built up an incredible tolerance to bacteria over the years, considering all the unconventional places her fork had been stuck.

When I look back over the Thanksgivings Marc and

I have shared with our respective families, I again see my upbringing in sharp contrast to the reality of my adult life.

There was the time that my brother-in-law arrived a half hour late for dinner, and when he pulled up to our house his car was on fire. Not smoking, mind you. It was on fire. Flames were shooting out the windows, and the tires were melting and boiling black smoke. Everyone was so accustomed to such entrances by this man that no one batted an eye. In fact, no one even got up from the table to investigate. He coasted to a smoky stop right in front of our house, came inside, asked for a pitcher of water, then returned five minutes later to join us at table.

There was the year that my sister showed up with her one-eyed Jack Russell terrier, who apparently had eaten something earlier that day that violently disagreed with him. Two carpet cleanings, new wallpaper, and one brand-new golf bag later, our house was habitable again. That same year, she asked me if I thought she should consult a pet psychic to try to make contact with her long-departed cat named Bear. She wanted to make sure he wasn't mad at her. I mean, how do you answer that? And, oh yes, this is the same sister who volunteers to bring one dish every Thanksgiving, then shows up two hours late with all the ingredients, unassembled of course. I think she has brought the same can of green beans to Thanksgiving every year since 1981.

The Thanksgiving that stands out most in my mind does so for a couple of reasons. Our teenage daughter had invited a new friend, a boy, to dine with us, and as always my husband and I were happy to entertain our children's friends. I come from a long line of "feeders." It's in my DNA to feed anyone and everyone who walks into our home, whether they're hungry or not.

The holiday meal was grand that year, even more spectacular than usual for some reason. We had family members from both sides with us for the holiday. The house was alive with jovial conversation and the mouth-watering smells that only Thanksgiving brings. Our daughter's friend was a very nice boy, very friendly and at-ease for a teenager. He fit right in.

When it was time for dinner to be served, Marc said Grace over the meal, and we all took our seats at the table. Everyone happily passed dishes and served themselves and others, commenting on how wonderful the food looked and smelled. My daughter's friend jumped right in, not being shy. I was so happy; Norman Rockwell, get your brush ready!

We were only a few minutes into this grand meal when I noticed an unusual sound, one I couldn't quite place. I looked under the table to be sure the dog hadn't gotten into something he shouldn't have. No, nothing there. I sat still for a moment, perhaps I was hearing a car engine outside, or perhaps someone had left a television on somewhere in the house. It was a low hum, sort of a grinding, wet-sounding noise. I soon realized that the sounds I was hearing were emanating from my daughter's friend--from his mouth, to be specific. I couldn't help staring once I had identified the source of the noise. It was mesmerizing, really, to watch this young man chew. He appeared to have taken a rather large bite of meat, one bite of each vegetable, and then stuffed in a roll to act as a stopper. As he chewed, this load of food rolled around in his mouth much like a commercial dryer rolls around a load of wet clothes. Hypnotic, yet nauseating. Even my daughter was staring in disbelief, and she usually finds nothing but humor in the most inappropriate things.

Then, right in the middle of answering a question someone had asked him about school or his family or something like that (I couldn't hear over the noise), our young guest sneezed. To give him credit, he did try to stifle the sneeze, but he had a bowl of sweet potatoes in his hands. I'm not sure, but I think he tried to tilt his head up and away from the bowl; it doesn't really matter.

When he sneezed, I saw a small object fly out of his mouth. It actually flew up into the air, then, apparently, fell somewhere onto the table. For a split second I sat amazed and thankful that he hadn't sprayed the five food groups all over everyone else. Without wanting to make a fuss or embarrass him, I discreetly looked in the general direction of where I saw the projectile land, not sure that anyone else had spied the unidentified flying object. I looked hopefully across the table, eager to find evidence that would mean that the foreign object hadn't fallen into a bowl of food or onto somebody's plate. Alas, no foreign object in view.

The young man obviously knew what I was searching for. When I looked at him, he was grinning and shrugging his shoulders as if to say, "Dang! What can I say?" There was a tooth missing from his grin. That tooth was somewhere in our Thanksgiving feast. My stomach rolled.

"Hey, can y'all help me find my tooth?" he asked, explaining that it had gotten knocked out years ago by a baseball and the replacement was a temporary never made permanent. Apparently, tooth mishaps were not foreign to this kid, as he seemed to be taking the whole incident in stride. To my horror, all of our children stood up and began digging around in the bowls of food to see if they could find the errant tooth. They used serving spoons to dig in most of the bowls, thank God, but still . .

Several moments into the search, a shout of victory: "Found it!" The rather large tooth was camouflaged in a dish of corn pudding. The young man reached into the dish and plucked the tooth from its hiding place. Expressing his gratitude to all who had helped in the search, he popped the tooth back into place, but not before our two youngest high-fived him and tried it on for size first. All this excitement got our dog Chester turned on, and he began dancing his particular version of the cha-cha with everyone who was standing. I sat there and watched my perfect Thanksgiving fade to a small dot, then disappear altogether. The little bit of food I had had a chance to eat threatened to return in a hurry.

My father, who was in his early eighties at the time, grumbled to himself about how the kids today had just "gone to hell in a handbasket." My mother-in-law busied herself trying to steer the conversation away from the tooth and the dog onto something more appropriate than the leg of a bystander. My daughter kept yelling, "No, Chester! Bad dog!" Apparently, this sequence of words acts as an aphrodisiac to certain breeds of dogs, so Chester carried on. My husband ignored the entire episode and continued to eat his food.

I ate very little at that meal, another Thanksgiving first for me.

I would be remiss if I neglected to tell you all about our youngest family member, Chester, the dog that played the brief but important supporting role in my Thanksgiving tale. He is a dog, but don't tell him that. In order to really appreciate his contribution to our family, you need a little background.

I think somewhere earlier in this book I made reference to the difference between how city Southerners and rural Southerners treat their dogs. My mother fell into the "city Southerner" category. When I was a child, we had a poodle named Prissy. Prissy enjoyed a much better quality of life than most humans. My mother made sure of it.

I was accustomed, then, to having a house dog and to spoiling it rotten. I was never much of a small-dog person, though. In my opinion, if you're going to have a dog, have a real one. A big one. They're not yappy and mean; they just love you no matter what. No matter what you weigh or what kind of mood you're in, no matter whether your house is clean or your bank account is full, a big dog loves you completely and isn't embarrassed to show it.

A few years ago, after losing our beloved golden retriever Maddie to a wicked cancer, I finally had the heart to consider getting another dog. I am a firm believer in rescuing dogs who need loving homes, so a good dog-loving friend of mine who often rescued lost or abused pets put out the word that the next retriever found that needed a home would be ours.

Before long I got a phone call. A small puppy, a stray less than two months old, had been brought to the local animal hospital. He was very sick and malnourished, but I fell in love with him the minute I saw him. He looked like a little buff polar bear with coal-black eyes and a perfect little nose. And he looked up at me as if to say, "Hey! You look nice! I want to live with you!" I was hooked. The veterinarian was convinced that he was pure golden retriever. As it turns out he is not, but I adore him anyway.

After a two-week stint at the animal hospital to get rid of all the worms, parasites, and other maladies the little guy had, our new puppy got to come home. My daughter years ago took on the responsibility of naming every pet we've ever had, and she didn't hesitate with this one. One look at him, and she pronounced him a "Chester." And Chester he has been ever since.

Now Chester, being street-savvy and having lived through God-knows-what in his young little life, knew a good thing when he saw it. And our home was a good thing. We had a pool, lots of running room, young children to play with, and what appeared to be an endless supply of food. Jackpot.

As we learned on that very first day that Chester came to live with us, he has an unusual way of showing excitement or gratitude. An embarrassingly unusual way, if you know what I mean--an embarrassing male-dog way of showing happiness. Am I making myself clear?

Through the years, and Chester is about five years old now, that embarrassing demonstration of affection has not abated. In fact, it's gotten worse because Chester weighs about seventy-five pounds, not the eight or ten pounds he did as a puppy. We have tried obedience classes (twice) to correct this. We have tried spraying him with water when he does this. We've tried shaming him, sharp tugs on a leash, and other negative reinforcements including a shock collar (which only turned him on even more), all to no avail. We ordered one of those doggie remotes you see on TV. It's supposed to stop any unwanted behavior immediately, just by pointing it at the dog and clicking. He ate it within twenty-four hours. The dog is hard-wired to rumba, and that's that. Nevertheless, Chester is a member of our family and therefore participates in our holidays and other events.

O, Christmas Tree

One of my family's most treasured traditions is the annual Christmas-tree search and purchase each year. Without fail, we make the pilgrimage the day after Thanksgiving. Living in suburban Atlanta, there aren't many Christmas tree farms near our home. We have gone to the same little fruit stand for our trees for more than fifteen years, and we'll continue as long as they're open for business.

Another tradition of ours is the conversation we have every year about the size of our tree. I remind everyone (including my husband) that a tree looks much smaller outdoors than it does indoors. I try to get them to understand that just because our family room has a twenty-two-foot ceiling doesn't require that we buy a tree that tall. And every year, my advice is ignored by everyone (including my husband).

About four years ago we had all of our children and several relatives with us for Thanksgiving. Of course, we were thrilled--the more, the merrier. Bright and early on the Friday after Thanksgiving, we all piled into our monstrous SUV and set out for the fruit stand. It was time to select our tree, and as always it would be the most beautiful and perfect tree on the lot.

As we approached the stand, we heard exclamations of approval from the back seats of the vehicle. Our children had already spotted a gigantic tree on the lot, and we were still a quarter-mile from the fruit stand. This tree was massive. As we got closer my husband's eyes widened, and he got that look on his face, that look that says, "Bigger really is better." It was the same look he had when we bought the state-of-the-art big-screen TV, the same look he got when he bought the turbo-powered lawn mower with a 64-inch-wide cutting path. I knew I was in trouble.

I launched into the "trees look smaller outside" speech before he even pulled into the parking space, but to no avail. No one was hearing me. They had homed in on the huge tree (I think it was a Sequoia brought in from northern California) and were walking toward it slack-jawed and hypnotized. There was no reasoning, no turning back. I tried again, in a stronger voice, to bring my family back to their senses, to caution them against selecting a tree that would take up our entire downstairs living area. They were still not hearing me. My husband had already made his way over to one of the workers who carries the trees to customers' cars. The guy laughed, asked him if he was sure that was the tree he wanted, then motioned to two other workers to help him load it up. I overheard one of them say that he couldn't believe they were actually going to unload that tree on someone. I think it was brought in as a marketing gimmick.

You know how they cut a thin piece off the bottom of the trunk to be sure the tree can get water once it's in the stand? The piece they cut off this tree was the size of a coffee table. The tree was twenty feet tall and very full. I think I saw a condor fly out when they shook it. It was a very big tree.

Once the trunk had been trimmed and the tree netted for ease of transportation, all three workers wrestled it onto the top of our SUV. They tied it down with twine, wished us luck, and left us to it. They were laughing among themselves and pointing at us as we pulled out onto the street to make our way home. I was more than a little nervous.

About a quarter-mile down the road, the tree started sliding. At first, it slid toward the front of the vehicle, completely blocking my husband's visibility. No problem; he just hung his head out the window and carried on. Then it began to shift sideways, hanging dangerously off the passenger side. I suggested we pull over so that we could readjust the tree, but I knew better. The more dangerous a driving situation is, the more alive he feels. He sees such scenarios as challenges, as tests of his survival skills. There was no way he was stopping. He forged ahead, while the children and I rolled our windows down to try to support the weight of the tree with our hands and arms so that the vehicle wouldn't flip. Our side of the windshield was completely blocked by greenery. I'm pretty sure we were driving on two wheels.

It took us about an hour to get back home. The fruit stand is only about three miles from our house, so we made pretty good time. We pulled into the driveway, and Marc and my son got out of the car first. They had to cut the tree free of the vehicle before the rest of us could open our doors. Marc and the kids were still ogling their find, exclaiming that it was the biggest tree they'd ever seen (true that) and that none of our neighbors would have one anywhere near as big (that too).

I began busily trying to clean the sap off of my car with hot water and a mop. My father was criticizing our purchase, waxing negative about the prospect of getting the tree into the house, even more about getting it to stand upright. Marc had already jumped into his truck to head for the local do-it-yourself home-improvement store to buy a new, sturdier tree stand.

Finally, not long before lunchtime, everything was in place, or, rather, out of place, and we were ready to bring the tree inside, to fill the living space cleared for its residence. It took five of us to do it, but we pushed and shoved and wrangled until the tree was firmly in the stand. I have to admit, I was as nervous about the setup as I was about the drive home. The new stand, despite its impressive dimensions, didn't appear big enough for the sequoia, but Marc insisted it was fine. The tree stand was one of those that swivels, making it easier to stand the tree up perfectly straight. That made me nervous too, but I didn't say anything. I didn't think any stand assigned the challenge of holding this tree needed to have moving parts. I glanced over at the box the stand came in; it said it was approved for trees up to ten feet tall. What? Ten feet? Even after trimming the trunk and cutting off the scraggly lower branches, this tree stood twice that height, easily. I did not feel good about this at all.

Surprisingly, the tree stood tall and straight after a little maneuvering. The children and I took over at that point, carefully stringing beautiful gold beads and lovingly hanging each heirloom ornament, with the help a tall step ladder and human anchors on both sides. My dad sat back and let us know when he saw a bare spot. My sister made mulled cider, and we all enjoyed a Christmas movie while we decorated. Oh, I do love Christmas. This tree really was a spectacular beauty, even if it did take up the entire family room and half the kitchen. I didn't even mind climbing the ladder to decorate the top half of it, and I am terrified of heights.

When we had finally hung the last ornament, I stepped back to admire our handiwork. Lights twinkled and reflected in the ruby-rich colors of the beautiful glass ornaments. Everyone voiced approval, and the children and I busied ourselves with putting away the storage boxes and cartons.

Later that evening, in that relaxing interim between dinner and bedtime, the whole family sat and talked. We reminisced about childhood days, exchanging stories about siblings and spouses that stirred laughter and stoked memories. It was wonderful, such a picture-postcard evening.

Then it happened, and with no warning whatsoever, other than a biblical rush of mighty wind, our beautiful Christmas tree, decorated so carefully and lovingly, crashed to the floor, burying two children and an old man in the process. Beads, glitter, and glass ornaments sprayed all over the room, as dangerous as any shrapnel on a battlefield. Our two dogs barked wildly, running back and forth from room to room to attack whatever had invaded their quiet little evening. Of course, Chester became over-stimulated and . . . well you know. My Aunt Louise, as proper and prissy as they come, will probably never set foot in our house again. Our youngest two children, frightened both by the commotion and the spectacle of the collapse of their Christmas tree, started crying uncontrollably. This made the dogs bark even louder.

Registering what had just happened and taking a quick inventory of the casualties, I looked over at Marc. He sat quietly amid the chaos, staring at where the tree had once stood and getting very red in the face. When you're married to someone long enough, you know what they look like right before they have a meltdown, and he had that look.

Once the dust had settled and the crying had subsided to random sniffles and hiccups, he stood up and cursed a blue streak that would singe your hair. Grabbing his hat, coat, and car keys, he stormed out of the house. He didn't say a word to anyone; he just left. My dad was still pulling icicles out of his hair and from the cuffs of his pants, shaking his head and muttering about poor planning. The kids looked at the back door that their dad had just stormed through, then back at me. The crying got louder, as they now tried to process where Daddy had gone. The dogs gingerly investigated the fallen tree, jumping back in alarm if something tinkled or jingled. The rest of the family just kind of looked around, dazed and as if they hadn't noticed anything out of the ordinary. They, too, wondered where my husband had gone in the wake of such a calamity.

About thirty minutes later, Marc walked back into the house in much the same way he had left, announcing that he needed a couple of people to help him carry something. My son and brother-in-law went outside to help him, more out of curiosity than a sense of duty, I'm sure. Even I was curious, and I was still in shock.

The three men pushed open the door and began turning and maneuvering a huge box, trying to fit it through the opening. They somehow got the thing through the door, then went back and brought in a piece of plywood that measured about 6ft. by 6ft. Without saying a word, Marc produced a drill, placed the plywood approximately where the tree once stood, and screwed it to the floor. Then he and his helpers began unpacking what appeared to be a large, heavy-duty fiberglass tub. They placed the tub on top of the plywood and screwed it into place. With sheer brute strength, energized by the adrenalin of seething rage, my husband picked up the mammoth tree himself and plopped it down into the bathtub. He bolted, screwed, strapped, and otherwise secured the trunk and bathtub, anchoring the tree into place. He was a man possessed. Then he went outside, dragged the garden hose in and began to fill the bathtub with water. He had not spoken a word since the tree had fallen, save the cursing.

Next, he screwed a hook into the family-room wall and strung heavy cable through it, wrapping the cable once around the tree. Our Christmas tree looked as though it had been executed for some capital transgression, but no one felt brave enough to say that aloud.

Standing back and admiring his ingenuity, Marc finally spoke. He announced to the room what a piece of crap the first tree stand had been. I bit my tongue, thinking it might not be wise at just that moment to remind him that the stand was out-muscled by about ten feet more tree than it was supposed to handle. And thus, we ushered in another traditional Christmas season.

The Redneck Riviera
(a Family Vacation)

Early in our marriage, Marc and I got the brilliant idea to take our whole family camping. That was during our spend-time-with-the-kids-in-nature phase, which lasted almost a week. We thought that if we spent time with them in nature without the distractions of television, phones, video games, and the like that we would form stronger, tighter bonds. We thought we'd be making memories to last a lifetime. And we certainly did.

I am not a camper. I am not the outdoorsy type at all. I do not like bugs, sweat, mud, humidity, cold, or excessive heat. I do not like not being unable to take a long, hot shower. I do not like knowing that there is only a flimsy piece of fabric between me and whatever roams the woods at night. In fact, in my opinion camping is to vacationing as bowling is to recreation. But the kids were very excited at the prospect of roughing it for a couple of days, so we set about preparing for an adventure.

Marc and I went to a local sporting goods store to

buy a tent. There would be a lot of us sleeping in it, so it had to be a big one. (As it turned out, a couple of cousins and our dogs were going to join us, too). Once in the camping section of the store, we came to understand, with the help of good merchandise display and an eagerly helpful young sales clerk, that we were going to need much more than just a tent. We bought lanterns, a cookstove, some camping stools, an air mattress, and various other accoutrements, to the tune of just over a thousand dollars. I instinctively calculated how many nights in a comfortable hotel that money would have bought.

When the big day arrived, the children could hardly contain their excitement. I am including Marc in that group of excited children. He is also a planner--very organized, very forethoughtful--and he soon had his truck packed to the brim with camping accessories. Everybody piled in--we had so many campers that we took two cars--and we were off.

We had pre-selected the campsite on the shore of Lake Lanier, North Georgia's loveliest, about an hour's drive northeast of Atlanta. The site offered a beautiful view of the lake, a couple of islands, and the property's four-star resort hotel, just across the water. I think I chose this site for that very reason. I could dream, couldn't I? If camping proved to be just unbearable, well the resort was not too far away.

Everyone had a pre-assigned job once we arrived, and the tent-pitchers set to work. We had two eight-man tents. I understand now why they're called "eight-man" tents instead of "eight-person" tents. Only a man could truly call those quarters livable. No self-respecting woman would have come up with that floor plan, either.

I went to work arranging coolers, hanging lanterns, setting the table, just trying to make the place look festive and homey. I even found some wildflowers that I placed in a cup and put on the picnic table. I must say, by the time everything was in place, we had quite an inviting little campsite.

In no time, we had hamburgers sizzling on the grill. The dogs were comfortably dozing nearby, and the kids were lined up along the shore, fishing and joking with one another. Maybe this camping thing would be all right. Maybe it wasn't going to be the nightmare I had imagined.

Just after dinner, Marc and the guys decided to build up the fire, to really get it going. I thought it was just fine the way it was, but I am not a man. Fire is a primal thing, and as with power tools and televisions, size definitely matters. The evening really was lovely, thoroughly relaxing, and I think I slept better that night than I had in a very long time. Besides, eyebrows grow back.

When I awoke the next morning, I was alarmed to find that I couldn't feel my legs or arms. They were frozen. Did I mention that we were camping during the kids' spring break, which falls in early April. Early-spring Georgia days can be seductively warm, but the nights are still very cool. I had forgotten about that. It took me forever to get the courage to peel back my sleeping bag and venture up the path to the community bathhouse. I carried my toiletries, some rubber gloves, and a gallon bottle of bleach with me. Already, the fun was wearing off.

As soon as I could move my extremities freely, which occurred about an hour or so after the trip to the bathhouse, I fired up our little cookstove to make breakfast--for three teenage girls, three teenage boys, a couple of young men, plus my husband and me. Breakfast took about two hours to prepare. I was starting to feel slighted and resentful.

After breakfast, the natives began to get restless. My son could be perfectly happy fishing for days on end, but the rest of the crew needed a little more stimulation. The older two boys, both nephews, decided to swim out to the island that was just offshore. The water temperature was probably in the mid-50s, and I tried to caution them about the wisdom of a swim. They would hear none of it, though. It really wasn't that far out to the island. How bad could it be?

Hearing a loud splash followed by a string of profanity that had to be my husband's handiwork, I abandoned the fruitless effort in support of good sense so that I could investigate. I came upon my husband just in time to see him pulling himself up out of the water, soaked from head to toe. Apparently, he had been relieving himself into the lake when the embankment gave way. He emptied his pockets--wallet, keys, cell phone--onto the picnic table, underlining each item with a curse word. He truly is a pro.

Once he calmed down and got changed into some dry clothes, Marc joined the conversation about the proposed swim. Of course, he encouraged the boys to go, to swim for it. What harm could it possibly cause?

In the meantime, my son and one of our daughters

got bored with fishing and broke out the golf clubs. They each chose a driver and teed up on the shore. My son is an avid golfer, and we learned that he had a natural talent for the game when he was very young. I wasn't fooled, though. This wasn't about practice. I knew exactly where this was going.

I'm going to make an observation about my sweet husband here that might sound critical, but I really don't intend it that way. He is a forty-seven-year-old child. He loves a laugh, a prank or a practical joke. He sees humor in just about everything, and in truth, he's usually the life of the party. I love all of these qualities, but I have to say that his love of laughter has sometimes caused him to make questionable calls with regard to the children. He has never done anything to harm them, mind you; he just always assumed the role of the good guy when they were young, the best friend, the one who never said "no."

All he had to do was take one look at the boys swimming out to the island, then look at our son and daughter driving golf balls into the lake, and I could see the light bulb flickering to life over his head. Without missing a beat, he grabbed his own driver, teed up a ball, and whacked it right toward the swimming boys. The kids still on shore thought that idea was pure genius, and they all followed suit. Soon, golf balls were raining down on the swimmers (numb and barely moving by now). Every now and then, a ball would make contact with its target and we'd hear, "Ow!" or "Hey stop it!" from the water.

I couldn't believe what I was seeing, and their dad was the ringleader. I told them all to stop, that what they were doing was neither safe nor responsible, but no one seemed to hear a word I was saying. Campers at sites on both sides of ours looked up to see what all the fuss was about. To my surprise, everyone thought that what they were witnessing was hilarious. They cheered the golfers on. I really was beginning to worry about the boys in the water. They had to be completely numb by now, their body temperatures dangerously low. They were moving slowly toward the island though, so I knew that they stood a chance. Soon, they both reached water shallow enough to stand up and walk. They trudged slowly up the muddy bank to reach the shelter of the trees. No sooner had the pair ducked into cover of the trees on the island than they came sprinting back out, screaming and running right back into the water. A Canada goose was hot on their tracks, hissing and beating the air with her wings. The boys were terrified. They were trapped between an angry mother goose and freezing water peppered with golf balls. They tried to flag down passing boaters, but no one in his right mind would have stopped to help those two.

Panicked, they began yelling at Marc for help. They were too cold to attempt to swim back. Marc, our children, and everyone else who had witnessed this ridiculous comedy were literally rolling on the ground laughing. In fact, the only people who weren't laughing were me and the swimmers.

Finally coming to his senses, Marc started talking to the boys, calming them down, and talking them through getting back to the safety of shore. He told them to look at the lake; more specifically, he told them to look at the brown line that ran from the shoreline to just right of where they were standing. He told them to walk over to that line, then follow it all the way back to shore. What my airheaded husband had noticed, whereas the boys and I had not, was that the water was only about a foot deep where the water looked brown, marking a shallows. They could have walked out to the island and back in the time it took them to swim through ice cold water, dodge whizzing golf balls, and avoid one very angry mother goose protecting her nest.

No future medical students, that pair, that's for sure.

Wrestling Down Demons

As I look back over these stories I've dredged up and recounted for your reading pleasure, I've come to realize that I myself may appear to be white trash to some readers. After all, you can't have this many close encounters with white trash and not belong to the same species, can you? I contend that yes, in fact, you can. It's not easy, but you can.

About twelve years ago, I married a man that is so unbelievably kind, generous, and just plain good that I still sometimes pinch myself for a reality check. All I saw was him, and I know from first-hand experience that his qualities are very rare. He is a wonderful husband and a terrific stepdad to my children. He is a man, however, who has "risen above his raising," and his family is a colorful one that has brought experiences to my life that I had never encountered before (the burning car and singing teeth, for example).

While being white trash has little to do with how much money one has, it has much to do with how little education one has. I could go on and on about why I believe this is true, but suffice it to say that the smaller your circle of experiences, the smaller your mindset. And by education, I mean either formal education or the better experience of travel. In addition you can mix with white trash and still maintain your proper Southern mindset. Then again, of course, you can succumb to the pressure and become white trash yourself. I think I am somewhere in between. I never thought I'd say that about myself until last summer, when we attended a professional wrestling event at the Arena in downtown Atlanta.

There, I said it. It's out in the open. We paid good money for the tickets, and my family and I went to see a professional wrestling event. Writing this admission just dredges up the shame and humiliation all over again, but if I'm going to point fingers and talk about white trash, I must be brutally honest.

Our best friends are a couple that Marc knew for years before ever meeting me. They are without a doubt the most colorful, interesting, entertaining two people I believe I've ever encountered. They are a study in contrasts, and they are one of those couples about whom you can truly say, They are meant to be together. On days when they aren't threatening to leave or even kill each other, I think they'd agree.

The husband is a graduate of the University of Georgia. He is intelligent, intense, and usually the life of the party. He is as good an example of a "Good Ol' Boy" as is Marc. His wife is without a doubt one of the kindest, sweetest women I know. Very laid back, she is loaded with common sense and integrity, and she has a healthy sense of humor. All of these qualities are musts for someone I call *friend*.

This couple has a ten-year-old son, and this boy is being raised in a sports-fanatic home. He loves football, wrestling, cage-fighting, you name it. The whole family got hooked on professional wrestling many years ago, and they are die-hard fans. You heard me.

They used to try to tell us about the drama and athleticism of professional wrestling. In truth, I would listen, laugh, and privately poo-poo the whole idea. I mean really, wrestling? I don't get it. The few times I'd try to watch it with them on TV, I couldn't get past the pathetic acting and manufactured drama. And I really couldn't understand beating the hell out of someone in a sanctioned fight, using a folding chair or ladder or whatever's within reach. Besides, in our family we have holidays for that.

Anyway, when our friends heard from TV ad that this big wrestling event was coming to Atlanta, they laughed and said, "Hey, we should all go." Marc and I didn't take them seriously at first, but we all have so much fun wherever we go, I finally said, "OK. Let's do it." So we bought tickets.

As the date of the event approached, I began to get a little nervous about going. Thoughts like, *What if someone I know sees me?* kept creeping in. Even sadder, thoughts like, *I can't believe my life has come to this,* were surfacing. I was not looking forward to going to this thing, but there was no backing out.

When we walked into the Arena and began searching for the right gate and then our assigned seats, I grew more and more amazed by the assembling crowd. The Arena was soon packed, standing room only. I was amazed. The few times I had seen wrestling on television, I always assumed that the people in the crowd were, I don't know, bused in from Alabama or Mississippi or New Jersey or someplace, or maybe I thought they just came with the show, like they were part of the set. Nope. The plain and sad fact is that every city on the wrestling tour contains huge numbers of wildly dedicated fans. They must total in the millions. Frightening I know, but it's true.

There were grandmothers with t-shirts featuring their favorite wrestlers in the Arena that night. One of them had her blue hair slicked back with baby oil. She wore fingerless leather gloves, and brass knuckles on her right hand. She gave me the once-over when I accidentally brushed her arm in the crowd, then she brandished the knuckles at me and curled her upper lip.

There were little children running around whose parents had bought them hundreds of dollars worth of wrestling memorabilia. Little Bubba, Jr., over there was pretending to beat the hell out of his little sister, while his dad looked on and gave him instructions on how to land illegal blows so the ref wouldn't catch him. There were fans who were all decked out to look like their favorite wrestlers, snarling and gnashing their teeth at imagined opponents. Hawkers were selling cotton candy at $22 a pop; the gauzy confection had been shaped to resemble the profiles of some of the regional wrestling favorites. And it seemed that everyone had a handmade sign, to be held up for the cameras when their guy got into the ring. I felt oddly unprepared. Was someone supposed to tell me that I needed a poster, some sort of visual aid?

We found our seats, and I looked around again in sheer amazement. The crowd was being whipped into a frenzy, with dramatic, poorly acted clips of previous events being shown on the huge overhead screens. Some fans booed their disapproval while others cheered in wild agreement.

To my horror, my girlfriend (not her son, not her husband) was one of those who was shouting. She was crazed, jumping up and down, and shouting expletives at the screens. Astounded, I tugged at her shirt in an attempt to get her to sit down, to snap out of it. When I finally got her attention and she looked at me, I recoiled. She had a look in her eyes that I had never seen before. She looked positively bloodthirsty. It was very unsettling. No, the fans are definitely not bused in.

The whole thing lasted about three hours, I'd say. It was like spending that time in some sort of time warp, a wrinkle in the universe, a parallel reality in which people have absolutely no decorum, no sense, no self-control. Now that I think about it, this event bore unsettling similarities to every wedding, funeral, or holiday I've described in this book.

That day was a turning point in my life. True, I had attended and survived one of the most wildly popular white trash hoe-downs known to man. And true, I got to see a side of my good friend that I had never seen before. I suppose it should have made me feel closer to her, but it didn't. It just puzzled me. I came away from that evening sadder and wiser. I realized that there are more wrestling-loving rednecks and white trash on this earth than there are people. I also realized that my friend had a whole other side I had never seen before.

Little did I know that the behaviors I saw her exhibit that night were only the tip of the iceberg. For now, suffice it to day that she also has a son who wrestles, but we'll get to that later.

It's How You Play the Game

∑⎯⎯⎯⎯

I've given this a lot of thought, and I've come to the conclusion that no book about Southerners, white trash, or rednecks would be complete without a section covering youth sports. The mere mention of youth sports is enough to raise the hackles of otherwise meek and unassuming moms and dads all across the South. This is probably true everywhere, but here in the South, and more specifically here in Gwinnett County where we live, Youth Sports is not a hobby or a pastime. It is capitalized, as you can plainly see. It is a religion, sanctified by the various governing organizations that run the leagues. In fact, Gwinnett County was named one of Sports Illustrated's Sportstown, USA communities offering families the state's best recreational sports and parks systems. Now it's wonderful to set the bar high for young athletes, and it's truly a blessing to live in a community in which the recreational facilities are top-notch. But I have to tell you, it does bad things to parents. Very bad things.

All of our children grew up involved in sports

beginning at a young age. They've played soccer, softball, football, golf, and my daughter cheered for many years. When I was a kid in high school, cheering consisted of wearing short, flouncy skirts, bending over as often as possible, and occasionally throwing in a cartwheel for good measure. Today, cheering should be an Olympic sport. These young ladies, in order to compete and earn a spot on a squad, have to learn to throw their lithe bodies in dangerous tumbling passes and stand three and four girls high on hard wooden floors. They have to be able to throw one another, catch one another, and deliver first aid to one another, all while never losing the smile or missing a dance beat.

I will go ahead and admit right here that I am not a fan of cheering. I never have been. My impression of the sport was always that it is not a sport at all; rather, it always seemed to me to be a popularity contest among mean, shallow, brainless girls. I now know that that is no longer the case. Girls who stick with the sport have to be in great shape, be committed to their sport, and above all, have parents with deep pockets. Astronaut training costs less than competition cheering, and is safer. Look it up. I read somewhere that more sports injuries, per capita nationally, take place among cheerleaders than among football players. I suppose the girls would not be nearly as entertaining to watch if they wore all that unflattering protective padding.

I'm going to delve even further back into my kids' sports histories to illustrate what I mean by white-trash and redneck behavior as exhibited in youth sports. I'll start with redneck behavior, since it's not nearly as offensive as white trash behavior.

Many years back, Marc's oldest daughter played softball. She was very good at it and eventually earned herself a full college scholarship with her skill. In order to be that good, you have to have played for a while. When she was, I don't know, maybe twelve years old, she played in a game that I will never forget. At that time I was not accustomed to youth sports in this particular county league. My two children had always played soccer in a very well organized league that demanded respectful behavior from both athletes and parents. When I met my husband and started attending his girls' softball games, I experienced what can only be described as culture shock.

The girls in this league were already performing at a professional level at age twelve or so. They were hurling the softball over home plate at speeds better than 60 mph., even then. Many of the players spit, scratched, punched, and cursed like the pros, too. Coaches shouted at the girls on a regular basis that it was not, in fact, how you played the game but whether you won or lost that mattered. One look at their parents, and you'd understand why.

Anyway, I was sitting in the bleachers at this memorable game. It was a warm spring day, and I had dressed accordingly, right down to my brand new designer sandals.

Marc's oldest daughter was playing first base, and the score was very close. I was surrounded by parents-- mostly moms, as the dads were too into the game to sit still. They paced along the fence line and motioned signs to the girls on the field. Most of them were sweating, veins protruding on their foreheads. Watching them was nerve-racking, so I turned my attention back to the game, sort of.

The mother sitting to my left had a huge tattoo on her massive upper arm and stringy hair pulled up in a sloppy ponytail. She wore motorcycle boots, a denim shirt with the sleeves cut off, and denim short shorts (bad idea), into which she was stuffed like a sausage in a spandex casing. She had facial hair and most of her teeth, and she was spitting pistachio shells randomly, most of them hitting my designer sandals. Every now and then, one would stick to my foot. I would have said something to the woman about her disgusting behavior, but my mother didn't raise a fool. Although I was getting a tension headache, I thought it wise not to mention the sandal thing to this woman. These particular shoes weren't really designed for running.

Every now and then, this mom would pipe up and shout a nugget of motherly wisdom to her daughter. Supportive phrasings like, "Strak 'er out Crystal! She ain't no good," and "Aim at'er head. That'll back'er off the bag," floated musically out over the field. I clutched my purse tightly in my lap and tried to make myself as small as possible. *How long do these games last anyway?* I kept asking myself. I secretly hoped she wouldn't notice me or my shell-covered feet.

The mother (no, make that grandmother) sitting to my right was gnawing on a piece of raw meat. I silently hoped that she was not a spitter as well. Then from somewhere behind me, I heard a man shout out to his daughter, who had just come up to bat. He said, and I quote, "Spank 'at tater, Holly!" Let me translate that for you novices who might be reading this. Literally, it means, "spank that potato." Figuratively it means, "hit the ball hard." His wife, the girl's mother, added for good measure, "Ram it down her throat." I was mortified. These were children playing a game, in a park!

As the years progressed, so did the obnoxious behavior. And that was among the girls. My son played football in the youth league and well into high school. He is a big guy, built for football with the heart of a lion and the disposition of a lamb. As a single mom, I could not fathom putting my son, my little baby, out there on the field with those deranged coaches. When my son played soccer, the fields were close enough to the football fields in the fall to hear those coaches yelling at the little six-year-old players. I mean, the county football league held combines to prepare and select players at that age. Some of the kids even had contracts. It's serious business here in the South, I'm telling you.

Of course, when I married Marc, he thought that putting my son in the area football league was a great idea. On the one hand, I agreed with him. I think children learn lifelong lessons by being involved in any team sport. Still, I had a hard time with it until I saw that my son could hold his own.

Over the years, I witnessed first-hand the most horrible, obnoxious, offensive behavior from the adults both on the field and in the stands. These are the transgressions that I group under the "white trash" label. I have seen coaches get into bloody fistfights right in the middle of two teams of young boys. I have seen a mother leap from the stands onto a coach's back, demanding to know why her son didn't get more playing time. I have seen and heard parents, grown adults, jeering at young children and shouting obscenities at them. It offended me then, and it still does today.

And there lies a problem, because a good friend of mine (she of professional-wrestling-fan notoriety) has turned into one of those moms. Off the field and out of the gym, she is as kind-hearted and considerate a woman as you'll ever meet. But put her son on the field or on a wrestling mat, and the gloves are off. I have actually seen her head spin around and foam at the mouth during a football game. I have heard her question a boy's genetic lineage during a wrestling tournament. I have seen her on her stomach on the floor at the mat on which her son was wrestling, screaming at the referee and her son's opponent with wild abandon. When these things happen, her eyes glaze over and become blank and dark, almost like she's one of the undead, but on crack. I have tried to pull her out of it, calling her name over and over and snapping my fingers right in front of her face, getting no response at all. She blacks out. She says she can't help herself, but I'm not sure what to think. She is actually cooking up a plan, a coup, right this minute to circumvent the state rule about not allowing glitter on posters at this weekend's state wrestling meet. (I did mention that her son is ten years old, right?). She plans to meet up with the other moms, prepare legal (and hopefully tasteful) posters, then sneak them home and cover them with glitter, i.e., tiny shards of shiny metal. The rule exists strictly for the safety of the young athletes. If the glitter gets on the mats, it can be abrasive to the skin, even dangerous to the eyes. When I explained that to her, she looked at me as if I had a third eye. I fully expect to see her on Saturday holding up a sign with a battery pack, complete with lights and a sound system. I think she hired a professional artist to paint her son's face on one side of the banner and a picture of herself mooning the crowd on the other. I would like to go and see the child wrestle, but I probably won't. Such behavior bothers me.

At any rate this conduct, I think, goes a long way toward explaining why kids burn out on sports so young. It certainly explains why some parents have been banned from their kids' games and practices in many leagues. And I think youth sports is just one more arena in which white-trash families shine. Any activity in which air horns and cow bells can be used is tailor-made for white-trash families.

The Family Reunion

Several years ago Marc's family called for a family reunion. My father-in-law was still alive, though frail, and everyone thought that a good old-fashioned get-together was just what the doctor ordered. Our children were young at the time, so we planned to take all four of them with us to Ohio. At this point in our marriage, I had only met the in-laws who lived close to us. I had never had the pleasure of meeting the Ohio clan, though I had heard plenty of stories.

My husband and I had made the mistake once before of trying to vacation with all four of our children. They were ages seven, nine, eleven, and thirteen at the time. We took them to the Gulf Coast of Florida for a glorious week at the beach. It was a nightmare, hell with a view, and I swore never to do it again. When news of the family reunion came, I thought to myself, *If they were that bad at the beach, what on earth will they be like on an Ohio farm in the middle of nowhere?* I was already dreading it.

The children, quite in contrast, were excited about the trip. They talked about it nonstop and even took the initiative to pack their own clothes. When the big day came, we all piled into the SUV at about four in the morning. The kids jostled for position, put on their headphones, and promptly fell asleep. Marc and I kicked back, enjoying the peace and quiet. In truth, I am a terrible driving companion, if "companion" in these circumstances means an alert respondent in and contributor to invigorating conversation. I usually fall asleep about twenty minutes into the trip. My husband loves this, because he can exceed the speed limit with reckless abandon, and I am none the wiser . . . until the cops inevitably stop us.

Our family has never traveled more than sixty miles round trip without getting stopped by state troopers or local police officers. My husband is of the mentality that speed limits are set and posted for the less experienced drivers of the world, not for skilled and accomplished drivers such as himself. He has a driving record that goes on for miles and miles; it takes cops a good half hour to read through it all on their computers before approaching our vehicle to hand out yet another citation of misdemeanor infraction of the Uniform Vehicle Code, otherwise known as a speeding ticket.

We had no sooner hit Interstate 85 here in Georgia than I fell asleep. About five minutes into my nap, I was awakened by sirens and the crazy flashing of blue lights piercing the predawn darkness--more than one squad car, from the looks of things. On this particular trip, my husband outdid himself, with a little help. My son, who was about fifteen at the time, and a couple of cousins had decided to follow in a separate car. There's something exciting about taking a trip without Mom and Dad in the car, even if you are following Mom and Dad's car.

Both cars were being escorted to the side of the road by some of Georgia's finest. When we were all safely pulled over onto the shoulder, I saw that there were not one, not two, but four patrol cars participating in this SWAT Team operation. What in the world? As I was coming to grips with just what was going on here, an officer approached the driver's side of our vehicle and asked my husband if he had been racing. *What?* I thought. *Racing?* Why in the world would he ask him that? Apparently, our car and the car full of young teen boys behind us were traveling side-by-side on I-85 going about ninety miles an hour. No matter how you slice that, it sounds like racing to me. I just looked at my husband, silently seething.

Now, my son is the kind of kid who would not, on his own, step outside the law if you paid him cold, hard cash to do it. He's just like that. I don't care how much fun or excitement other people tell him he can have; he will do the right thing every time. It's one of the things I love about him. His cousin, however, loves to test boundaries, expecially legal ones. Anyway, you can imagine how my son reacted when the car he was in and his parents' car were surrounded by cop cars, lights flashing, sirens blaring.

Marc knew that my son would be very upset by all this, so he proceeded to step out and check on the boy. That was a mistake.

The second Marc opened his door, more cop cars materialized out of nowhere, surrounding us on all sides. Then I heard a voice over the loudspeaker, "Sir. Step back into the vehicle NOW." Was that a helicopter overhead? Were those search lights?

Another officer approached the driver's side of our car, asking again whether the two drivers had been racing. My husband replied that no, of course they were not racing. Couldn't the officer see that both cars had young people in them? This was simply a little family trip, completely innocent. In the midst of all this, our youngest daughter leaned forward and asked the officer to smile, that she wanted a picture of this incident for her scrapbook. I was mortified. I was surrounded by inmates. I was fighting a losing battle for sanity. My whole family had gone crazy.

About an hour later, when all the cops had left and all but one TV news van had packed it up, we were back on our merry way, headed north to Ohio. I was furious with Marc. We didn't speak for another fifty or so miles (which, I later understood, was actually a payoff for him, not a punishment). When we finally did speak, I launched into yet another lecture about responsibility and setting examples for young people, especially our own children. I thought the speech was well organized and made perfect sense. All he heard was "blah, blah, blah." His only response to my speech was to say that he had always driven that way. Period. That was it. What does that mean, exactly? I could have strangled him.

Despite getting off to such a rocky start, we did arrive in Ohio in time to check into our hotel and get settled before heading out to the farm. We had booked several rooms, and all three of our girls were staying in one room, at least initially. When I got news that they had ordered room service twice, as well as an iron--to be used as a weapon, mind you--we made other arrangements. Once we had reorganized room-occupant logistics offering safety for everyone, we embarked on our journey to the farm.

Now the farm at which the reunion was being held belonged to my brother-in-law, Dick, and his wife, Theresa, proud owner of the full-length beaver coat. I was really looking forward to seeing them. I had always enjoyed their company. They were hard-working, responsible, yet funny and adventurous people. It was the rest of the family that I was apprehensive about meeting, and all because of the stories I had heard.

Don, my other brother-in-law, and his girlfriend were also at the reunion. Although no one knew it at the time, Don's girlfriend was married to another man. She always went to elaborate lengths to explain inconsistencies in her life history, which she shared and edited often. This woman was scary, in a fatal attraction, boiled rabbit, acid-on-the-paint-job kind of way. She sulked and stomped through the entire weekend, taking every opportunity to belittle Don and generally to make people feel uncomfortable. She was a lot of fun to be around.

Not long after we arrived at the farm, the alcohol began flowing. I feel I need to explain something here, lest you think that I am an anti-drinking fanatic. I see absolutely nothing wrong with having a drink or two (or even three or four, if you're not driving or responsible for young children). I have done it myself on occasion over the years. What I have a problem with is the person or people who drink as though they are in a race to see who can consume the most, the fastest. I have a problem with those who chug to see who can become the most obnoxious, the loudest, the most offensive. The champions of this ignoble pastime are those who do that, then get behind the wheel of a car--not merely disgusting but incredibly selfish, irresponsible, and, well, criminal. OK, I feel better now. Let's move on.

Theresa and I were sipping a cooling strawberry margarita on the front porch, enjoying the late May breeze, when we saw a cloud of dust on the horizon. As the cloud blew ever closer, we could see that the dust was being kicked up by a caravan of eight or so cars. "Oh no," Theresa said. "They're here." "Who?" I asked. "Who's here?" No one was there to answer my question, though, because everyone was running around the house hiding silver, hiding the liquor, hiding anything of monetary value. Mothers picked up their children and held them tightly; dogs ran for cover. Apparently everyone knew who "they" were except me.

After about ten minutes, "they" all pulled into the long drive that led to the farmhouse. The cars kept coming. When they all had come to a stop, the doors flung open, and out "they" piled. I will not use the family's last name here, but it was Flo's entire bloodline. Everybody. The people kept coming and coming, like one of those little circus cars that looks like it holds two people and forty clowns pile out.

For a split second, the two genetic branches faced each other, no one saying a word. I couldn't tell if they were going to fight or embrace. You could have heard a pin drop. Then, as if on cue, everyone crossed the imaginary line and began hugging and kissing. Exchanges like, "Oh, it's been years!" and "You haven't changed a bit!" were volleyed back and forth. Some linked arms and walked off toward the picnic tables. Others found shade under the big oak tree out front and started reminiscing about old times, about the days when they were carefree kids.

Theresa came up from behind and asked me whether I was ready for a refill. She was sneaking the "good stuff" and saving it for a select few; everyone else could drink cheap beer. In fact, the eight carloads of relatives that had just pulled up had all come empty-handed, a practice I'm told is a regular occurrence with these folks. Looking around, I saw that each and every one of them had at least one beer in each hand. I quickly tried to recall the stories I had been told over the years, to try to match faces with anecdotes.

That was Carla, the worn-out looking woman in cutoff shorts and a tube top, polishing off her fourth beer. She and her husband, the guy belching and scratching his armpit, had both just gotten out of prison, and just in time to welcome their great-granddaughter into the world. Carla was thirty-nine, and her husband looked to be in his eighties. He was actually forty-two. One had been convicted of welfare fraud and the other for possession-with-intent-to-sell. Five years previous, I wouldn't have known what either one of those legal terms meant.

The great-granddaughter had been born to a thirteen-year-old child, and Carla couldn't have been more proud. She recounted the story as proudly as most parents would recall their child's college graduation. My husband pulled all three of our daughters close to him, instinctively protecting them from whatever seemed to be in the water up here.

The guy over there talking carburetors with some man I hadn't yet identified was cousin Human Torch. We talked about him earlier, remember? He was guzzling beer and asking my son to pull his finger.

Area fifty-one was there, too. He had gathered a crowd under the oak tree and was regaling them with some story about his miraculous survival of a contaminated canned-food incident, or did it have to do with a banana peel on a porch step? All I know for sure is that it ended with him anticipating a huge insurance settlement, buying two corvettes, and moving to Florida. Check.

Cousin Kathy was there. Physically, she looked pretty good except for the fact that she had bleached her hair pretty much white and was slurring her words, slobbering when she laughed. Unfortunately, she picked me to be the one she brought up to speed on her love life. Apparently, she was seeing a married man who didn't seem to want to leave his wife. "You're kidding," I replied, scandalized. "Don't they usually leave their wives for the convenient, secret, easy mistress?" She slobbered that no, they don't. She slobbered that she deserved better and wondered whether she could go back to Atlanta with us to get her life back on track? At just that moment, I got a pretend call on my cell phone, and I went inside to secure some privacy and a little breather. No such luck.

The younger kids were inside, and ours had joined them. That alone was alarming, but as I got closer to where they were sitting, I heard one of the Ohio cousins telling our thirteen-year-old how she was dating a twenty-something "dude" that makes the best fake ID's in the state. Instinctively, I snatched up our daughter and told the other kids to come outside with me for a family picture. It was the best I could muster under the circumstances.

I hustled all the kids outside and looked around for a safe place. Everywhere I looked, people were chugging beer--yes, even kids who were not old enough to be drinking at all. It was, evidently, a family tradition, so all I could do was to warn mine against it. I had once made the mistake of saying something to the family matriarch about minor children drinking every time the family got together. I thought my remarks would be received as care and concern. Instead, I got an offended stare. Like I said, beer consumption is a rite of passage. It signifies a coming of age.

Anyway, as families all over the world do, eventually the men separated into groups to play horseshoes or just to shoot the breeze, and the women sat in the shade and discussed pregnancies, marriages, divorces, and any juicy gossip that had just been uncorked. I made sure that all three of our daughters sat next to screaming, crying babies, just for safe measure.

As the afternoon stretched into evening, Dick built a huge bonfire. We all pulled our chairs closer, as Ohio nights are chilly well into June. Once the fire was blazing, that's when the drinking kicked into high gear. At some point, one of the guys suggested a friendly game of corn hole. You heard me. Corn hole. Instinctively, I looked around for our children, ready to grab them and run if needed. Nothing good can come of something named "corn hole," even if it is a game.

For those of you who don't know, corn hole is actually a game of beanbag toss. You know the game; you toss a bag of beans (or dried corn, in this case) from a distance, aiming for a little hole in a board. I know how it sounds, but I think you have to drink for a while before it makes sense. I gather that you have to drink a lot for it to be fun. Me? I can't even get past the name.

My husband, always a lover of a good game of horseshoes and, as it turns out, corn hole, grabbed my hand. He wanted me to go with him and watch. I'm going to tell the truth here; he had had a lot to drink. It was easier to go with him than to reason with him. The game had been set up behind the barn. It was dark by that time, so the guys had pulled up two trucks, intending to shine headlights onto the area where the game was being played. Of course, because they were all plastered, one set of lights was aimed more or less out into the cow pasture, the other somewhat more toward the nearby barn, neither directly illuminating the game, the players, or anything relevant in the vicinity. That was the first thing I noticed. The second is still burned into my memory, probably forever.

One of the guys already playing corn hole was married to . . . Oh, I don't remember whom he was married to; it doesn't matter. What matters is that just as I turned at the barn's corner he was bending over to pick up the corn bags. I was staring a little too directly at his backside and was met with a good six inches of crack shining for everyone to see. And I'm not talking about crack, the drug. I'm talking rear-end crack. I immediately looked away, embarrassed and a little nauseated. Then, when it was the other team's turn to throw the bags, I witnessed the same thing--a lot of crack. I mean, do you say something? Do you politely look away as if nothing is showing? Or do you walk away? I chose to walk away. As I walked past my husband, who had also shared some crack with the gathering crowd, I gave him a pleading look that said, "Isn't it time to go back to the hotel, honey?" He didn't take the hint. As I was walking back to the bonfire, with a little more intimate knowledge of the in-laws than I cared to have, I noticed I was walking a path that the cows seemed to favor as well. I was ankle-deep in manure. Great. Just great.

Made in the USA

I mentioned earlier in this book that a very close relative of my husband has passed away. In truth, several close relatives of his died in succession, one after the other. It was very sad, and my husband had a hard time coping with each devastating loss.

One of those was tragic death of his oldest brother, Dick. He died suddenly one afternoon of a heart attack. Just like that, he was gone. He was a good man, respected in his community, and loved by many. As a young man, he served in the U.S. Navy; so of course, his funeral was a military affair. As is customary, his wife, Theresa, was given the flag that covered his coffin once the ceremony was over.

Months after Dick's burial, Theresa (she of beaver-coat fame) bought a triangular shadowbox in which to store and display the flag. To her horror, she found a tag on that flag that read, "Made in China" while she was carefully folding Old Glory one last time. She was outraged, furious at what she considered to be a slap in the face of every American soldier who had served this country.

So she stewed and stewed . . . and stewed, as only a woman can do. One day she vented her disgust to her mother-in-law, who also happens to be my mother-in-law. Once the mother-in-law got wind of this offense, she began telling all the relatives. It was only natural, then, that my husband's brother Don eventually got wind of the news.

Now, in the interest of decorum and respect for my husband, I will not go very deeply into this particular brother's shortcomings. This is the brother who drove for years on a suspended license and knew every nook and cranny of every jail and prison in the entire southeast, the one with "bad luck," the one the cops "picked on" incessantly. Suffice it to say that he made a hobby of exaggerating, building mountains out of molehills, so to speak. He loved being the center of attention and was a pathological liar. I will stop there, not because I couldn't go on . . . and on, but because he's dead, having passed away not long ago. Let it lie.

Spotting an opportunity to right an insufferable wrong and, coincidently, make himself look important and well-connected, Don called the news department of a major Atlanta TV station to report the fact that the Chinese were churning out flags for American soldiers and undercutting good, hard-working American flagmakers with their red white and blue wares. It was blasphemy, and he wanted something done about it.

As luck would have it, a local investigative TV reporter took the bait--hook, line, and headline. Because this seasoned reporter has a son in the military, this story hit home with him. He called Theresa at her home in Ohio and made arrangements to interview her at our home when she came to visit the following week. Wonderful! Finally, this insanity would be exposed and stopped! I, for one, felt energized and relieved.

Theresa did come to Atlanta that next week, and the night preceding the Big Interview she decided for some reason to take the flag out and to show me the offending tag. She carefully pried the glass cover off the shadowbox and unfurled the flag along the length of my sofa. She felt along the edges for the tag as she went, hoping to come across it before having to unfold the entire flag. Nope, not there. Must be along another edge. She finally stretched the entire flag out across the sofa, and I saw a flutter of panic on her face.

"I know it's here. I've looked at it a thousand times!" she explained, laughing nervously and practically unraveling the flag in a desperate attempt to make the tag appear. I glanced at the shadowbox, and stuck to the wooden back of the box was a sticker that read, "Made in China." Uh-oh. I thought, "Surely not."

"Aha! Here it is!" she exclaimed triumphantly, pinching the tag discreetly sewn into the selvage of the fabric. "Can you believe that?" I leaned over to read the print. "Made in the U.S.A. by the X Company." I have omitted the company name here--it's in Alabama, by the way, as the label made clear--strictly out of embarrassment and, to tell the truth, out of a sense of gathering doom. I asked my sister-in-law, in a tone of voice I hoped disguised my building doubt, whether there's an "Alabama" in China. That sense of doom was gathering because on the next day the entire Atlanta viewing area would be up in arms about flags made in China and flagrantly draped over our soldiers' coffins.

The look on her face was that of pure confusion, flustered astonishment, and I knew that, once again, things didn't look good with respect to family notoriety.

"It was here Carole, I swear!" she sputtered. She was holding the sewn-in tag, but nowhere on it was China mentioned. I pointed to the "Made in China" sticker adhering to the shadow box, but she was not deterred. She swore that she had seen the offending tag on the flag. Fighting back the natural urge to panic, I spoke as calmly as I could in order to keep her from panicking. I had to try to work through this, not only for Theresa's sake but for my own. The thing is, I am a reporter here in metropolitan Atlanta, too. Somehow, I saw this fiasco bringing my fledgling journalism career to a screeching halt.

I thought it prudent to check out the company whose name was on the tag. I was hoping it was actually a clever front for the Chinese manufacturer. A brief Internet search revealed that not only does the U.S. company indeed make U.S. flags but also that the people who do the work are disabled U.S. citizens. Great. I pictured a red, white, and blue SWAT team swooping down on, into, and through the offices and work-floor operation of this small but proud manufacturer, cuffing innocent disabled people, while a news crew rolled film of the entire event.

Obviously, someone had made a mistake. In fact, several someones had made a string of mistakes. An investigative reporter would be at my house the next morning to do a story about the imported flags, and I just knew that all they would tape would be my heartfelt apology about the entire matter. I would never again be hired in the wide world of Atlanta reportage.

Theresa called the news station to explain what had happened. She didn't speak to the reporter directly but left a courteous and comprehensive explanation on his answering machine. She assured me that she had nipped the episode in the proverbial bud. That's when I began to get nervous.

The next morning, she and I left the house early. Understand, that our departure had nothing at all to do with the fact that the news crew had been scheduled to be at our house at 9:00 a.m. sharp, but we made a point to be gone by 8:45. I took her to my favorite coffee shop, and we sat outside sipping coffee and chatting. Then my cell rang. My husband was on the other end, and his voice sounded stilted and rehearsed. In fact, it sounded as though he had an audience. He asked where we were and when we planned to return. Pretending not to know by now that the reporter and his cameraman were setting up shop in my living room, I nonchalantly responded cleverly, "We're shopping. I don't know how long we'll be gone. Why do you ask, Honey?"

Silence.

I tried a different tack. "Is something wrong? Do you need something?"

Silence.

Theresa asked if I was talking to my husband and whether the investigative reporter was at our house. I nodded "yes."

To her credit, Theresa took the phone and asked to

speak to the reporter. She explained what had happened, embarrassed by the entire matter. I am please to report that the reporter was kind and gracious, chalking the mistake up to Theresa's grief.

If he only knew.

PDA

When I was almost finished with this book, Marc and I took a break from our respective workdays to enjoy a lunch date with each other. Even after all these years, I still look forward to unexpected, stolen afternoons.

Anyway, there we were sitting in one of our favorite little dives. It's kind of a sports bar/theme restaurant, but it has great food and a friendly staff. Marc and I were chatting about nothing in particular, going over the past events of that day and those yet to come, when out of the corner of my eye I spotted a person who appeared to have two remarkably distinct colors of hair. I kept getting glimpses of brown-red-brown-red. Odd, I thought, so I turned my attention to that table to get a better look.

As it turns out, what I was seeing was not one person with two colors of hair but, rather, two people so intertwined that they appeared to be, uh, "one flesh." There was so much full body contact and friction making between the two, I expected a fire to spark spontaneously under the table (figuratively speaking, of course). The pair looked to be in their early twenties and apparently oblivious to the fact that they were in a public place--a restaurant, no less. They would have looked more appropriate between the sheets than in a restaurant booth. I was transfixed, both annoyed and fascinated, with their passion and poor taste.

The first thing I do when faced with such situations (and it seems that I'm faced with them a lot) is try to remember back to the day when I was just as recklessly in love and oblivious. Then I remember that I never was. Don't get me wrong. I love my husband fiercely. I am completely in love with him. But even twenty or thirty years ago, I never loosened up enough to try to conceive a child in an eating establishment during the lunch rush. Or, if I did I've repressed it.

As I was saying, just when I thought I had wound up my thoughts on pretty much every major white-trash misbehavior, I was reminded of one of my biggest pet peeves, and that's the public display of affection. I call it PDA, for short.

To a true Southerner, privacy and all things private are of the utmost importance. Take finances, for example. One never, and I mean never, asks someone how much money he makes. It's impolite to ask someone how much something he owns costs (from shoes to vacation property), and the question of how much debt someone shoulders, or is considering carrying, is completely off limits. It's considered in very poor taste to spend ostentatiously or to proclaim blatantly one's ability or inability to do so. To many, these proprieties seem silly. (I know, I've been told.) But again, there is an unwritten code of conduct here in the South; some lines simply are not to be crossed, some subjects never broached. I know, I know, all regional cultures can make the same claim, but here in the South we have our own way of making and breaking these basic codes of conduct.

The expression of unbridled physical lust is another of those private areas, no pun intended. Brown and Red over there at Table 4 were not the least bit concerned that others around them were trying to eat, trying not to stare and failing miserably. In fact, the entire time that my husband and I were having lunch, Brown and Red were so impossibly entwined that, in the event of an emergency, the Jaws of Life couldn't have pulled them apart. I believe they were actually licking each other's tonsils when our check came. I wanted to walk up to their table and ask them to name the child after me, since I witnessed its conception.

I have witnessed way too many public displays of others' physical urge to reproduce, and every one has made me uncomfortable, as if I were watching a low-budget soft porn play. Even when I was in college, that glorious time in a person's life when free thinking and liberality are supposedly at a peak, PDA made me feel uncomfortable.

Believe it or not, I have witnessed PDA at both weddings and funerals. I've witnessed it at holiday gatherings, small children's birthday parties, and at church picnics. I've witnessed it in the Women's Pavilion at the local hospital, while I was there coaching my girlfriend through the birth of her son. Talk about irony.

While I have many recollections of tasteless expressions of PDA, I will focus on one poignant story. I have no doubt that you, too, have been discomfited by others' embarrassing display of overeager affection, so you'll get the general idea.

The account I'll share is a page ripped from a family friend's funeral years ago when I was in my early thirties. The deceased was a good friend of my parents; he and his wife and my parents used to play cards together, they took trips together, and his wife even babysat us during that period when my mother worked in the late '60s.

When the poor man died, my siblings and I were expected to attend his funeral, and we did, and so did many other former kids from my youth. Seeing people from so many years past was both nice and a little sad. Neighborhood kids we used to play with were there, of course adults by then, and some with children of their own. I was especially happy, at first, to see one man in particular; his family's house had been right across the street from ours when we were growing up together. He was my age, and we had shared many games of hide-and-seek, walks home from school, and so much of the other stuff with which kids used to fill their days before the technology revolution. It was good to see him.

His name is Scott, and Scott was recently divorced. That marriage had produced two little hellions, both of whom he had brought to the funeral home with him. He had also brought his new girlfriend, who looked to be just a bit older than his children. Scott was obviously enamored with this woman, as his eyes never left her for one second. They didn't leave her when Thing 1 and Thing 2 were climbing all over the casket. They didn't leave her when his two little horrors were dodging in and out of other rooms, with other grieving families saying goodbye to their deceased loved ones. Those two children were wildly out of control, and

Scott was unaware that they were even in the building.

I had had enough when the younger of the two, a boy of about four or five years old, stood beside the casket wiggling flowers under the deceased's nose to see if he could make him sneeze. This was followed by both of them bouncing golf balls and trying to get them to land in the casket after the first bounce. I stood there in disbelief while the widow just looked at the kids and cried, too grief-stricken to stop the shenanigans herself. As I recall from the days when she babysat us, she could swat a rear end from across the room, and with the best of them. She obviously was not on her game that day.

I looked at Scott, who was gazing into his underage girlfriend's eyes. When he started groping her in the corner, I snapped. Taking matters into my own hands, I marched over to the two little darlings and snatched both of them up by their ears (my trademark move when my own children couldn't seem to interpret what I was saying to them). The children howled and screamed all the way across the room and into the next. Scott was still completely unaware, his tongue exploring the back of the girlfriend's skull from the inside, and his hands exploring Lord knows where. I caught a quick glimpse of my father sitting in the corner, laughing at the entire spectacle. No help there.

I escorted the two screeching brats into an adjacent room that was completely empty, save for an open casket and an elderly male deceased resting inside. Then, with my face uncomfortably close to theirs, I very distinctly uttered the best threat I could think of on such short notice. I vowed to stuff them both inside the casket with the old man resting just beyond my pointing finger and close the lid if they didn't stop screaming. They stopped, looking at me with wide eyes and mentally marking their first encounter with a crazy woman or, worse, corrective discipline. I then proceeded to explain to the two about being quiet and respectful and settling down long enough for their dad to pay his respects. (As I said, this speech was completely off the cuff. They were already showing more respect than their father.)

Sniffling and hiccupping, they both agreed to calm down and find a seat. Then I took both of their hands and walked quietly back to the other room with them, praising both of them on the great job they were doing. Then a wave of guilt washed over me, and I slipped them each a ten dollar bill in an effort to counteract the effects of the casket-stuffing threat.

Once the two were seated on a loveseat out of the way of traffic and the gathering crowd, I began looking for Scott. Ah, there he was, still groping and exploring in the corner. Someone could have walked off with his two little angels, and he'd be none the wiser. I marched over to him and surprising even myself, smacked him in the back of the head. "Where are your children?" I asked. It took a minute for him to register both the smack and the fact that he did, in fact, have children. "I . . . I . . . I . . ." he sputtered. On a roll, I smacked him again. That one was just for my own entertainment. "Where are your children, Scott?" I asked again. His preschool girlfriend was looking at me just like the kids had moments earlier. Apparently, I had the honor of being her first encounter with a crazy woman, or worse, too.

Answering my own question, I told him that his children were sitting quietly across the room. I told him that they were doing so because I had put an end to the terror spree they enjoyed earlier. Grabbing his blow-up doll's hand and calling for his children to "come on," he shot me a look that, believe it or not, said something like, "Thanks for interrupting. I was about to get lucky." Without uttering a word, the four of them marched out of the room and out of the funeral home, but not before both brats turned around and stuck out their tongues at me. What so terrifies me about this episode is I am forced to accept the fact that by this time those two hellions are old enough to vote.

A White Trash Checklist

Not sure if you or someone you know is white trash? It's kind of like birdwatching. Grab your binoculars, and use this handy checklist:

Tattoos

A person with tattoos is not necessarily white trash, and a person without body ink may very well be. Confusing? Yes, I know, but let me see if I can explain. Strategically placed tattoos on a woman--those on the (very) lower back or on one or both breasts--are a pretty reliable indicator that the bearer is white trash. In fact a tattoo on a woman's lower back is often referred to here in the South as a "tramp stamp" or a "Panama City license plate." Oddly enough, the presence of tattoos on a man has nothing at all to do with his social classification. He likely served in the armed forces at some point.

Piercings

The jury is still out on body and facial piercings because people from all walks of life and most social classifications can be seen walking around maimed and stapled--by their own choice, I mean. I think the issues involved in piercing run much deeper--psychologically, I mean--than whether one might be considered "white trash."

Tobacco use

Follow me here, because this can get tricky. A smoker is certainly not necessarily Southern and may not be white trash, trailer trash, or a redneck. A smoker is merely a person who is engaging in a deadly hobby, an addiction. A man who dips or chews tobacco (I will not get into particulars here in the interest of decorum) is likely a redneck and very possibly white or even trailer trash. A woman, however, who dips or chews is definitely a redneck and most likely white trash. A word of advice, though: Do not tell her this unless you're sure you can outrun her or unless you're well-insured (*but see also the section below entitled "Female Brawlers"*).

Profanity

As one who respects the language, I place great importance on one's use of words and where and when one uses them. I don't think I'll ever get used to hearing profanity being tossed about as if it were nothing. Again, the prolific use of profanity does not necessarily mean that the user is white trash, but statistically the odds are very good. The casual slinging about of offensive words demonstrates a complete lack of consideration for others unfortunate enough to be within earshot. And as we all know, lack of consideration means the absence of manners--another predominant white-trash characteristic.

Year-round Christmas decorations

We've all seen the house that's still decorated for Christmas when it's time to hide Easter eggs. How about the house that still has lights up on the Fourth of July? More than likely, those perennially lit homes belong to white-trash families. Of course, extenuating circumstances may have prevented the homeowner from packing away all the decorations in a timely manner, but probably not.

While I'm on the Christmas decoration bandwagon, let me address the type of decorations white-trash families tend to display every year. The flashier, the louder, the more obnoxious the decorations, the more they appeal to white-trash families. One year, I actually saw a monstrous four-wheel-drive truck parked on a family's front lawn. It was completely covered with twinkling lights, and the tires had been wrapped with chasing lights. In other words, the artist was trying to make the truck look as though it were moving. Get it? Right next to the truck was a yard sign that read, "FIRST PLACE--NEIGHBORHOOD HOLIDAY DECORATION CONTEST." I have seen a blow-up Santa riding a camel (I think there's blasphemy in there somewhere), and I have seen plastic elves running their cards on an enormous blow-up credit-card machine. I have seen tacky wire Christmas trees that flash different colors to the tune of your favorite canned Christmas carols. I have seen the images of snowflakes projected onto the front of a house in an attempt to mimic a snowstorm. The spectacle more closely resembles a bad LSD trip. Yes, Christmas in the Deep South can be both beautiful and horrifying.

Automobiles in the front yard

Much like furniture and appliances on the front porch, cars and trucks parked in the front yard of a home are an unmistakable white-trash red flag. In fact, if one or more of those autos is sitting up on blocks or looks as though it's being cannibalized for spare parts, you can bet your life that you're looking at a white-trash dwelling. Take a picture.

Female brawlers

My mother taught me from a very young age that young ladies do not physically fight. Period. In the white-trash culture, however, women will brawl for any reason given half a chance. I'm talking the last piece of cake, the last can of hairspray, or the last cigarette in the pack. You name it, they'll fight over it. If the dispute is over a man, forget it. Two white-trash women will fight to the death if the prize is male. I'm not talking about the slappy, hair-pulling kind of fights you see on the Oxygen channel, either. I'm talking punching, kicking, biting, bludgeoning--epic battles almost to the death. Oh, and another note: The more worthless the man, the bloodier the fight. Worthless men are plentiful in the land of white trash, and white trash women are powerfully attracted to them. I would suggest, unless you're in peak physical condition, that you not flirt with a trashy looking, lazy man. His name is probably tattooed on the arm of a toothless female prizefighter who chews tobacco.

Partially dressed, unsupervised offspring

Anyone who's ever shopped at a big-box discount retailer has encountered the mother with a toddler in tow, that toddler dressed in nothing but a diaper. If it's wintertime, he'll have on a diaper and a t-shirt. His little feet are invariably bare and filthy, and he may very well have a red, high-fructose-corn-syrup sucker in his mouth, or a baby bottle filled with RC Cola. If the toddler has an older sibling, that child is likely zipping up and down the aisles with the baby in the shopping cart, completely disregarding innocent bystanders. Occasionally, Mom will scream an idle threat in the general direction of the children's last known whereabouts, but to no avail. You are witnessing the shopping habits of the genus *White-Trash humanus*.

Clothing

I hesitated to include this item on my checklist. I respect individuality and personal choice as much as the next person, and that respect extends to a person's manner of dress. I have already admitted to being a less-than-snappy dresser. I had to admit to myself, though, that there are a few repeating similarities that must be addressed, all of which likely add up to the wearer being white trash.

First let's take a look at women. White trash women have an affinity for tight-fitting clothes. If the woman is sporting fat rolls, the clothing is even tighter. White trash women believe that ten pounds of themselves really does look better when crammed into a five-pound garment. Oh, and bras are optional, always.

The white trash male is typically dressed by the white trash female. Look for flannel shirts with the sleeves cut off, anything that screams NASCAR or a favorite brand of tobacco, and of course motorcycle logos. T-shirts with profane words or references to women's anatomy scrawled across the front are another favorite.

What's yours is mine; what's mine is mine

True white trash is of the mindset that everything that you own is theirs to take, use, steal, sell, break, and/or lose. Further, neither an explanation nor an apology is required once your property has been lost, stolen, or broken. It's part of the "I don't feel like working, so you owe me" mentality commonly shared among this social subculture. The attitude of expectation never stops, and it applies particularly to your money--e.g., cash required for bailing relatives out of jail or paying monthly bills that your white-trash relatives can't seem to predict coming every month.

The absence of manners

If you've checked this list and still aren't quite sure if your subject is truly white trash, dine with that person. Always going back to the premise that manners are a demonstration of one's consideration for others, it just follows that the lack of manners is a white-trash characteristic. I'm talking about all manners, but for the immediate purpose let's focus strictly on table manners (or the lack thereof). Really bad manners are one of my pet peeves and provide a sure-fire way to find out exactly what you're dealing with.

Either wrangle an invitation for yourself or invite the subject in question to dine with you. Be sure to suggest or serve a piece of meat that should be cut before ingesting, such as a steak or a baked chicken breast. Be sure to serve a drink. If you're dining at home, serve the entrée and side dishes from serving bowls.

Watch the subject. Does he cut a small bite of meat from the larger piece, place it in his mouth and chew with his mouth closed? Probably not white trash. But if he stabs the entire piece of meat and holds it up to his mouth to gnaw on, that's one in the "yes" column.

How does he chew? Can you hear him from the back bedroom on the third floor? If he chews with his mouth open or, even worse, if he chews and talks at the same time, food spewing intermittently onto the table and into his lap, probably white trash.

When he takes a drink, does he pick up his glass with his left hand, thus leaving the right hand free to continue gnawing and shoveling? Nauseating, isn't it? Perhaps he loads up his mouth with half-masticated food, then gulps enough liquid to soften the mass. Maybe he doesn't pick up the glass at all, but leans over to slurp whatever liquid he can coax up from the rim with his lips and tongue. Could be white trash.

When you pass him a serving bowl piled high with, say, mashed potatoes, is he content to let you hold the bowl while he digs in, licks the spoon, and decides whether he wants more? Pass him a basket of bread. Does he let you hold it while he fondles each piece before selecting one? Check. It's official.

Lastly, steer the conversation right up to, but not quite into, an inappropriate topic. Does he take the bait and run with it? For instance, is he more than happy to give you a play-by-play account of the last time he had the stomach flu? How about the last time he had a cold? Better yet, does he share with you the intimate details of the last time he "got lucky?" You are dining with white trash, my dear.

To conclude: People who don't bother with table manners are not concerned with how disgusting their habits appear to others. Not until I was well into my thirties did I fully comprehend that consideration for others is not resident in our DNA; it must be taught. Therefore, manners must be taught, and learned. Too often they are not because, in most cases, white trash begets white trash.

What Now?

I have thought for most of my adult life that it was "us" and "them." I had this idea--what with my upbringing, my education, and my elitist attitude--that I was about as far from being white trash as possible. But as I read back over the stories I've shared here, I am beginning to see that I might just be one of "them," at least sometimes. I might be white trash, or pseudo-white trash. I don't feel like it. I don't think I look like it. Nevertheless, I certainly seem to spend a lot of time thinking about it, don't I?

I suppose that the lesson I've learned throughout my life--I'm relearning it every day--is that people are who they are, warts and all. As a rule, they can't be pigeon-holed into this category or that. Even the simplest of us is a complex being. I have to say, though, that I have found priceless humor in everyday situations, in the otherwise mundane exercises we perform day in and day out.

People are on their own paths. They have their own agendas; they have their own goals, their own ghosts. Isn't it a good idea to sit down every now and then, lower your guard, and laugh a little, even at ourselves? I believe it is, and I thank the family and acquaintances and flat-out strangers who have unintentionally contributed to this book. You have taught me to laugh--at you of course--but also at myself, and in spite of myself. I'll leave you to wonder whether I'm scratching my armpit or burping while I'm laughing.

Carole Townsend

Carole Townsend is a columnist for the Gwinnett Daily Post, the second largest newspaper in Georgia and a freelance writer whose articles have appeared in Ladies Home Journal and Teen Magazine. She has been described in her writing style as a cross between Lewis Grizzard and Erma Bombeck. She has established a reputation as one of the up-and-coming writers in the humor genre and has earned a national following.

Southern Fried White Trash is her first book. Written in her unique humorous style that has earned her a readership around the nation for her eclectic wit, the book is a collection of humorous but real life stories that have happened at weddings, funerals, and holidays and other family gatherings. Townsend writes in a style that sees the humor in situations and lets the reader know that it is OK to laugh at life's absurdities. Townsend and ***Southern Fried White Trash*** have been featured in the Los Angeles Times, CNN, and numerous television and radio appearances across the country.

She is busy writing her next book, ***Red Lipstick and Clean Underwear,*** that is a *"painfully humorous survival guide to successfully navigating life as a woman."* ***Red Lipstick and Clean Underwear*** takes a humorous but incisive look at "how women were taught to view and prepare for life as young girls, vs. the reality of being a woman and handling all that we do, every day, day in and day out. As adults, we are expected to handle, juggle, balance, earn, mother and be caregivers." It will be released in June of 2012.

Townsend is a graduate of Lipscomb University in Nashville, TN, with a degree in psychology, and holds a Masters Degree in Journalism. Prior to becoming a full-time writer, she Directed Marketing for The Baer Group, LLC and Western Digital Corp., both in Atlanta, and a major international software manufacturer.

She resides in Lawrenceville, Georgia with her husband , four children and two rescue dogs.

Follow Carole on Facebook, (Carole Adams Townsend) and Twitter (@caroletownsend).